Fighting
MY INSTINCTS
A GAY CONVERSION THERAPY DROPOUT STORY

ANGUS MACGREGOR

Please feel free to send me an email. Just know that these emails are filtered by my publisher. Good news is always welcome.

Angus MacGregor - **angus_macgregor@awesomeauthors.org**

About the Publisher

4Fun Publishing, a member of **BLVNP Incorporated**, 340 S. Lemon #6200, Walnut CA 91789, info@blvnp.com / legal@blvnp.com
NOTE: Due to the highly emotional reaction of some people to works of erotic fiction, any email sent to the above address that contains foul language or religious references is automatically deleted by our anti-spam software and will not be seen. All other communications are welcome.

DISCLAIMER

Fighting My Instincts

A Gay Conversion Therapy Dropout Story

By: Angus MacGregor

Chapter 1
Descent into Madness

There is nothing quite like hearing your mother scream to take the edge off your boner when you are just about to unload your nuts into your boyfriend's ass. Laying here in this shithole room I can still hear her shriek reverberating in my head. "Oh my God! My baby is getting raped!" But it didn't take long for her to realize it was her baby doing the raping, although it's pretty hard to rape the willing I've always heard. And boy, was Peter willing! Ten seconds later, she was throwing the entire laundry basket full of socks and underwear at my head and running out of the room with her hands over her head screaming for my dad. By the time he got there, Peter and I had just about gotten our pants back on but one look at our flushed faces and sweaty chests must have filled in all the blanks for him. He didn't say anything, but his face spoke volumes.

That night, the inquisition took place around the dinner table as I pushed Brussels sprouts around my plate and felt like I was eight instead of eighteen. My mom's voice was so shrill, I am surprised the neighborhood dogs didn't just all descend on our house and devour all of us. My dad didn't say much, he never did. He's been like that my whole life. I really wish he would speak up and maybe man up a bit too. I wouldn't want him to push my mom around but if he could just grow a pair and speak up for me once in a while, it would be ahmazing.

Okay, so I might as well fill in some blanks for you since you are reading this and obviously are curious as to how in the world going to gay conversion therapy could make me turn gay. It's a fascinating tale, one that I think you will find funny and goddamn sexy. So before we get to the shrieking around the dinner table, let me catch you up on the first seventeen years of my life.

I was born Dylan Thomas Cappaletti in 1996 to James and Starla Cappaletti of the huge metropolis of Sheridan, Oregon. The tiny town of 6,000 was mostly known for two things: a federal prison and Phil Sheridan Days. Phil Sheridan was a Civil War general who came out west after the war and got an even better job of rounding up the local

Native Americans onto shitty reservations until they just gave up their rights in the 1950's and stopped being Indians at all. In the 1980's, the local tribe found their pride and voice again and Republican Jesus Ronald Reagan restored the tribe who built a big casino and are currently at work getting the white man to pay back what he owes, one pull of the slot machine handle at a time. The town still celebrates their heritage by using the name of the only slightly famous person to ever live in the town, much to the local tribal people's chagrin. They attempted to truncate the celebration back to "Sheridan Days," but most of the dick people in town just kept calling it "Phil Sheridan Days," so the tribal council just gave up and decided the money they were making made up for at least some of the insult.

I was the baby of the family. My older sister was almost ten years older than me. My older brother, Derek, definitely had middle child syndrome and spent most of his time being a class-A douchebag to me and my friends. I pretended I hated him all the time and we rarely hung out or did anything together unless forced. Secretly, I loved him and longed for his approval and attention. We shared a room together until he left for college when I was thirteen. During that time, I spent plenty of time wrestling around trying to keep his ass or sack out of my face. He was hugely stronger than me so mostly I lost those battles. Plenty of rainy weekends found me pinned down on the bed with my brother's crotch pressed against my face as he rubbed his erection all over my head. Most of the time this was with his tighty-whities on, but sometimes, I got the full Monty version, his big furry balls landing in my mouth and nose. I told my dad about it. I think my dad must have known my protestations were half-assed. He always ended up asking me did I really want him to punish Derek for being a bully or was it just brothers playing around? The fact was, I loved every minute of it.

I secretly enjoyed watching Derek parade around our room in his shorts and naked as well as his nightly masturbation rituals to which I was a bystander to. Derek had so much fun spanking his monkey, I discovered I could do the same at the ripe old age of ten, thanks to my genetic big blast of testosterone and the hairy heritage of our Italian-Irish ancestors. My dad's head was bald but more than made up for it on his chest, belly, ass, crotch and legs. He had a smattering on his back but not the big Neanderthal look that some old guys have. Derek sported a thick crop of dark brown fur under his pits and on his belly that trailed down to a soft brown triangle surrounding his mighty penis. So when I found the first few hairs on my balls when I was eleven, I somehow knew I was ready to go. But even though I was so eager to talk with my brother about my feelings, somehow down deep inside I knew he wasn't interested in being my mentor.

When Derek wasn't there, I would sometimes find a dirty pair of his underwear or one of his jocks and slide it over my face while I rubbed my dick. Now before you laugh and tell me what a little perv I am, just remember, I felt really alone and isolated even though I wasn't an only child. In my very religious home, no one ever spoke about sex or the body changes of puberty. My only instruction came from the unlikely source of our pastor's son, Ben, who was three years older than me. I began to hang out with Ben more and more, finding his quirky sense of humor enjoyable and his easy way a relief from my family. He took me under his wing, taught me video games, taught me about popular music and more importantly, The Beatles and other classic bands. My mom was more than willing for me to spend a great deal of time with him since it made her feel that much closer to the pastor's family. We began to do sleepovers with one another, staying awake late at night talking and laughing. I was surprised to find that Ben's vocabulary took on a decidedly saltier tone when it was just the two of us. Like me, he matured early and was seemingly a pro when it came to beating his meat and talking about sex. Unlike Derek, he seemed to enjoy the mutual exploration that I was longing for.

One winter night when the wind was blowing hard and rain was coming down mixed with snow, Ben had come over to spend the night since Derek was spending the weekend hunting with some friends from school. Ben came over to my house and we had a great time playing and goofing off until we were ordered to bed by my mother. After turning the lights out, the dim moonlight filtered through the window and lit up my room in silver. I was lying in bed quietly playing with my penis while watching Ben pump his hand up and down under the covers when he surprised the crap out of me.

"Hey, Dilly (his pet name for me). You still awake?"

"I am now."

"Bullshit, you were awake. I see your eyes open over there, watching me."

"I'm not watching."

"Double bullshit." Ben sat up in bed and for some reason looked around the room. "Come on over here."

"Why?"

"Just come over here, Nutsack," Ben ordered, but not in his usual mean tone. I shrugged and headed over to his bed and climbed in beside him. A quick peek when the covers came back confirmed my new big buddy was indeed big and plenty excited. I settled in beside him and wondered what was about to happen, expecting a naked wrestling match was very probable.

"So you've seen your brother do this for a long time, I bet. You know what I'm doing?"

"Yeah."

"What?"

"Jacking off," I answered feeling my mouth go dry and my penis get hard.

"Yeah, okay. Do you know why I do it?"

I looked at my friend and watched him pull the covers down, exposing his erection and his hand slowly stroking his teenage cock that was big and leaking.

"No, not really. Cause it feels good?" I ventured.

Ben chuckled. "Fuckin' A, little buddy. It feels fucking amazing."

"Why are you saying the F-word all of a sudden? I bet your dad would freak out and go and grab a belt or something." (The pastor, like my mom, was a big proponent of corporal punishment for boys.)

"Fuck him," Ben hissed defiantly. "Here, give me your hand." Ben took my hand and wrapped it around his penis. It was hot and soft and firm all at the same time. Sliding my hand back and forth felt like magic. He pushed the covers down and looked at my dick. "Yeah, I figured you were hard too. Feels great, don't it?"

"Yes," was all I could say. His hand expertly fondled and stroked me, incorporating my balls and dick into one mesmerizing how-to instruction session.

"Shit, you already have hairs on your dick. You know what that means?"

I shook my head and stared at his penis growing even harder in my hand.

"It means you probably can already shoot your cum."

My blank expression told him I had no idea what he was talking about. Ben rolled his eyes and launched into a teen version of the birds and bees, with a heavy dose of boners, semen, and the wonders of the pussy. I listened with rapt attention feeling my balls tighten and draw up to my belly as he continued to stroke and talk. Finally, he pulled his hand away and gripped his own dick and stroked quickly until he was red-faced and out of breath. Suddenly, he groaned and a thick white silvery ribbon of semen shot from his penis and splattered on his belly and balls, drops landing on my cheek and lips and on my dick. When Ben finished he sighed and lay back grinning at me like an idiot.

"Pretty cool, huh? Wow, I shot my load all over you too." He scooped up the drops on my dick and oddly enough, licked his fingers like a boy licking frosting from the mixer beaters. "There's some on your lips. You can taste it."

I stuck my tongue out and tasted the salty-sour fluid and made a face. "It's not very good."

"Yeah, well. It's supposed to go in a girl's pussy, not your mouth most of the time."

"Why do you put it in there?"

"God, you are so dumb. You fuck your dick inside her hole and shoot your cum in there so you can make her have a baby. If you don't want a baby, then you have to wear a rubber."

"Rubber?"

"I'll show you later. Okay, now your turn. Let's see if you really are old enough to shoot your nut."

With that, Ben spat into his hand and began to pump his fist up and down on my dick, rolling his thumb over the tip. I could feel his breath warm and wet on my belly and balls as he stroked me. I watched a drip of sweat from his upper lip drop down to my dick as he jacked me.

"Spread your legs apart and play with your butt hole while I'm doing this. Get your finger wet and slide it in."

This was incomprehensible to me but I obeyed. As Ben jacked me, I slid my finger into my asshole and felt the tingle build within my belly. Finally, my balls drew up and I felt the quickening in my gut until finally, my very first orgasm exploded all over my older friend's face. Ben's mischievous grin. Two drips of pearly white boy cream hung from his chin.

"Damn, Dilly. I can't believe you can jizz already. That is pretty cool. Well, guess I know what you're gonna be doing every night like me now," Ben said with a quiet laugh.

"Do you jack off a lot?" I said in awe of all that was happening.

"Oh yeah. You will too now. How did it feel, bro?"

"Like my heart was going to explode, then like a golden shower."

"Er, that's kind of something else, big guy. Better keep that to yourself. Okay, you are making me too hot so get out of my bed." Whatever older friend-bonding was going on was definitely over.

A few weeks later, Ben slept over again when Derek was away for the night with friends. After the lights went off, he summoned me over to his bed once again. We went through the same rituals, more or less, only this time, my friend produced a foil packet from the pocket of his discarded jeans lying in a heap on the floor. He proceeded to show me the intricacies of rolling a condom onto your dick. I watched with rapt attention, my senses and my penis fully aroused.

"I probably shouldn't ruin one of these for you, but I like the way they feel on my cock when I blow my load. I steal them from my dad's dresser so I can practice. So see, you start up here at the top and when you get it all set, you roll it down. Leave this tip part all loose and baggy. I used to think you were supposed to cram your whole dick into that nipple part, but you're supposed to let it be loose so it catches your gravy. Then once it's on, you just slide into the girl's pussy and fuck away. Some guys even slide it into the girl's butthole, so it's really nice to have the rubber on then."

"Why would you do that? I thought you put it inside the girl to have a baby. Do you have one if you put it in her butt?"

"No, stupid. It just feels good."

"Can you put your dick in a boy's hole too?"

That was pretty much the last time my dad saw me naked and the last time he talked to me in any form or fashion about sex. My sister went to college and Derek moved into her room and from them on, I was on my own as far as sex education went. Like Ben prophesied, I began to jack off religiously, practically every day. And as I grew, I found that I enjoyed fantasies that included me and friends from school. Sometimes, I looked at photos of naked girls or girls and guys fucking. It was interesting, but I noticed I was mainly looking at the dicks. In fact, the photos or videos of girls where you were looking into the insides of their vaginas totally freaked me out. All that weird frilly shit falling out of there, ack…it just didn't appeal to me at all. It reminded me of the man-eating plant from "Little Shop of Horrors." And yes, I like all things Broadway and musicals, so fuck you if you want to bust my balls about that since it is so stereotypically gay. It's still fun and I don't care if you think it's cliché. I happen to really love college football too, so eat me.

Now where was I? Oh yes, back in high school…sexually frustrated, curious, and utterly lost. I was in journalism, drama, and band. I was a top student and even quasi-popular in some circles. Like most other gay guys then, I was totally in the closet. In fact, I didn't even know there was a closet. My mother kept telling my dad that I was just a late bloomer and didn't chase every skirt in town like my brother. I was pretty sure that was not the case. She fixed me up with a couple of girls for some disastrous dates. I have fun with them going out to eat or to the movies. I would even hold their hands and kiss them a bit. But when they inevitably want to make out more, take off their top or slide their hand down my pants, I freeze up. One girl, Becky Mitchell, actually took my dick out and jacked me off in the car one night, telling me how big my cock was and all that. But at the end after I came, she could tell I was freaked out. She even asked me if I thought I might be gay. That was the first time I even contemplated it. She was sweet and kissed me (and the tip of my dick) and told me it was no big deal if I was and that some guy would be very lucky to fall for me one day. That little sentiment and affirmation changed my life.

My senior year was great in practically every way. I felt more settled and comfortable in my own skin. I was looking forward to college and getting away from the parents. My mother's ultra-conservative political and religious views were smothering and my own feelings of certainty that I was queer (as she always put it) were becoming clearer. This all came to the dramatic conclusion that started this story off when new boy, Peter Stone, moved from Stockton, CA up to my tiny Oregon hamlet. He was a trombone player like me and was the first to ever challenge me in band. For the first time ever, someone actually beat me in a competition and I got bumped to second chair. But instead of being furious, I was intrigued. We began to hang out after school, playing video games, listening to music, admitting that we loved theater and Broadway musicals and acting. Peter was definitely more outwardly flamboyant than I was in every way. He dressed more stylishly, was overly dramatic with his mannerisms, and felt at home with the girls and alienated from the boys. All of them except me, that is.

On a band trip back from a competition, we sat on the back seat together. It was cold and rainy and we had a blanket to keep us warm. As we rode back, Peter fell asleep on my shoulder. I thought about waking him to tell him to get off, but the fact was, I loved the way it felt. Our legs were pressed together and I had a raging hard on. My hand lay against his and I softly rubbed my fingers against his hand. He didn't seem to mind or respond. After some time, I slowly moved my hand until it lay in his lap. We both had on sweat pants and I could feel the warmth radiating from his crotch. As I moved my hand and rested it in his lap, I could feel his penis, hard and pulsing, against my touch. I looked across the aisle and Robby Middleton and Kyle Goss were covered up as well. It might have been my imagination, but it looked for all the world like Kyle's hand was moving up and down under the blanket while Robby laid back in utter nirvana.

Peter coughed and I moved my hand. He didn't wake up, he just readjusted himself in the seat and settled back against my shoulder. I looked over at Kyle who was smiling, but not in a dickish way. I could tell now that he was definitely jacking Robby off. He even lifted up the blanket and I watched his hand slowly stroke Robby's thick erection. Kyle looked at me and gave me a thumbs up and pulled the blanket down. I smiled and slid my own hand back into Peter's lap only to find he had pushed his sweatpants down underneath his balls. I froze for a moment and then felt his hand touch mine and move it to his boner and wrap my fingers around his shaft. He snuggled closer and I began to masturbate him along with Kyle. Kyle smiled as he watched and he pulled the blanket up again. I brazenly did the same and his eyes widened. Peter's cock was rock hard and leaking precum by the gallon. We continued to milk the boys sitting beside us until I saw Robby stiffen and raise up in the seat. A thick rope of silver shot from his cock up to his chin and Kyle's cheek and lips. The boy continued to stroke him, slowing down as we drove on. Kyle's head lowered for a moment and I stared as he swallowed Robby's penis and licked it clean. Robby looked over at me, momentarily surprised, but once he took in my hand stroking Peter, he grinned and did the thumbs up himself. Peter's head moved and he watched the scene unfold across the aisle. I could see him smile and he turned back to me with a look of affection and arousal. With the softest grunt, he released his nuts all over my hand and his t-shirt. Kyle and Robby grinned and watched me slowly stop my stroking, wondering what to do with the mess. Kyle actually reached across the aisle and scooped up some of the semen and licked his fingers clean. Stupidly, I did the same, tasting Peter's cum, hot and sour on my tongue. How could this be happening, I wondered? These boys I had known my whole life were gay or at least acting like it? It was almost too much. Peter's hand moved to my lap and gripped my erection. I knew he wanted to jack me off but I was too freaked out.

He smiled and moved his face right against mine. "I'll come over next week and give you a turn," he whispered. I felt my dick swell even more.

And he did just that. The following Monday he drove me to my house. I introduced him to my mom who seemed genuinely pleased to meet him and instantly invited him to church. I noticed her scrutiny, however, and it unsettled me. I had seen Ms. Judgmental too many times before. We grabbed a snack and headed to my room to study for a test. We had barely made it in the room before Peter's hands were gripping my ass pulling me toward him. Our lips met and I felt an electricity that I had never felt before. My mouth opened to his tongue at once, the scratchy mustache rubbing against my lip. My cock was instantly hard. I broke away briefly and wedged my desk chair under my doorknob while I watched Peter push his pants and shorts down to the floor, his boner wet and dripping. I followed his lead and soon we were naked and kissing on my bed. I felt his hands rub and probe my belly and ass. He pulled my ass apart and his fingers teased up and down my furry crack as we kissed. My hand gripped his penis and stroked it as we kissed. Before I knew what was happening, Peter slid down and swallowed my penis all the way to my pubes. I groaned and involuntarily began to hump his mouth. I repositioned myself and opened my mouth to allow his cock to slide inside. It was utterly delicious and completely perfect in every way. We sucked and fucked one another in the mouth until we unloaded our balls in thick, creamy blasts. Afterward, we lay naked on the bed, fondling one another, kissing, and grinning like idiots. I knew that two doors down, my mom was busy working on dinner and here I was, fornicating or something, with another boy, just like the men of Sodom. And I had never been happier.

For the next few months, Peter and I spent as much time as possible together. His parents seemed perfectly happy for us to hang out there most of the time, which made it more comfortable for me. At school, we acted as straight as we could. But I could feel his gaze on me. Sitting together at lunch, his hand would lightly touch mine under the table and I would harden instantly. At morning break, we would head to the bathroom at the same time. Standing beside him, seeing his erection peeking out from under his shirt, would make me lose my mind.

Sometime around Easter, we had Peter's house to ourselves on a Friday night and he penetrated my ass for the first time as we lay in front of the fireplace. Losing my cherry to Peter was almost spiritual. He spent so long eating out my hole, I thought I was going to cum. Then he eased his penis inside, slow and steady. The pain was momentary and he waited for my muscle to relax before sliding the rest of the way in. He plowed my boy pussy deep and hard as I lay on my belly, letting him breed me in long, powerful strokes until he filled me with his seed. Later that night, I lost my other virginity, fucking his sweet ass as he bent over the back of the couch while we watched "Back to the Future." I had never felt anything so glorious.

And so, we fell in love and fucked the living daylights out of one another as often as we possibly could until the fateful day. Peter's family was having guests stay from out of town and there was no way for us to find any privacy. I knew no one was going to be around that afternoon, so we found ourselves in my bedroom. We sucked on another until we were ready to explode before I flipped Peter over and mounted him like a bull. My cock was sliding in and out of his lubed hole just like always when my mother walked in the door and ruined my world.

"What do you have to say for yourself, young man," my mother huffed as she sat at the table, arms folded, fuming.

I looked at her in bewilderment. I didn't know how to tell her I was in love, that I felt more alive than I ever had, that sucking cock was better than life itself. "I don't know," I said quietly.

"That Sodomite friend of yours has bewitched you, I can see. He put some spell on you and made you perform those disgusting, sinful acts."

"No he didn't. It was as much my idea, Mom."

She slapped me with all her might, making my head ring. I held my face and stared.

"Sheila!" my dad said standing up and grabbing her hand before she could hit me again. She sobbed softly and sat down, hiding her face in her hands. She wiped her face and looked at me with fierce anger.

"No son of mine is going to be a queer," she said. "You did not learn that filth in this house. How long have you and that faggot been fornicating?"

Her words were so hateful I didn't know what to say. Anger was building inside me as well. "For a long time and it was wonderful."

Her eyes flew open and she lunged at me with her nails out like talons to claw my eyes out. Once again my dad stopped her.

"That's enough, Sheila. For God's sake. He is our son, whatever else is going on."

"No son of mine would perform those acts, like a dog," she hissed.

"Actually, your son did. I've been on my knees servicing him, mom. He has penetrated me like I was a cheap whore. Your little boy loves cock, mom!"

My mother shrieked and tore at the air in front of my face with her claws. My dad held her back. "Dylan, shut up and leave the table. Go to your room!" My dad ordered as he tried to restrain my mother from obliterating my face. I went to my room and fell onto my bed, screaming into my pillow. At that moment, I know I could have really hurt my mother, I was so angry. I didn't want to feel like this. I am a peaceful person. I just wanted someone to believe in me, know that I really did know what I was doing. And not fill me full of all their bigotry and intolerance. I think I fell asleep because sometime later when it was dark outside, I was shaken awake by my dad. I opened my eyes to see his tight, weary face above mine. I sat up and nervously looked around for my mom.

"She's not here. It's okay," my dad said reaching out to hold the side of my face with his hand. It was warm and dry and I think it might have been shaking a bit.

"I'm really sorry, Dad. I never wanted…"

"I know, Son. Wish it had been different. But the cat's out of the bag now, and I'm afraid there aren't a lot of choices here."

I sat up and leaned close to my dad. He put a strong arm around me and pulled me close. "What does that mean? Are you going to kick me out of the house?"

Dad smiled weakly. "Of course not. But I have to tell you, your mother won't be able to let this go. She thinks you are sick, confused, or possessed or something. She believes you can be fixed…you know, converted."

"Dad…I don't think it works that way."

My dad hugged me close and sighed. "I don't know too much about any of this, but your mother has talked to the pastor and he is recommending sending you to "Straight Ahead". They think it can help you start to like girls and everything."

I laughed right out loud. "Don't you think if shit like that worked, a million gay guys would just sign up and get all changed? It's not like they wake up one day and think, 'Hmm, life's not very exciting so I think I'll start sucking dicks."

My dad actually chuckled and reached up and tousled my hair. "I know this is a long-shot son, but wouldn't you like to be normal?"

"I don't know, Dad. If it makes me an intolerant asshole, I'm not sure I do." My dad looked sad, wounded almost. I could tell he was feeling lost and ganged-up on just like me."

"Look, Dad. I am confused about all this. I didn't expect to have these feelings. It would be fine to just wake up and say that I get boners every time Brittany Spears bends over on a video. But so far, that hasn't happened. But if it means this much to you, I will go to this stupid place. I'll even try to believe it. I'll do it for you...not her."

My dad hugged me close and I heard him sniff. "I love you, Dylan. No matter what, I love you son."

And that's why I found myself driving toward Central Oregon to the lovely campus of "Straight Ahead" to get the gay in me prayed away. I didn't have much faith and even less that a stupid conversion therapy camp would turn me into a pussy-loving macho man. But as I drove up Highway 22 to the Santiam summit, one thing did pop into my mind: there were going to be a lot of guys at this place who have been sucking dicks for a while. And a big grin spread across my face.

Chapter 2
Taking One for the Team

I checked in at the front desk of "Straight Ahead" along with another bewildered looking guy about ten years older than me. He seemed mortified to be there and particularly nervous. I tried to make eye contact but he avoided my gaze. He was ahead of me but I could tell he didn't want to talk with me around. I finally just asked if he would like me to check in first and he shook his head and smiled weakly.

The man behind the desk looked like some straight-laced Mormon bishop. His hair was parted so precisely, it looked like it had been done with a razor. "Welcome, Dylan. It's great to meet you and have you join us at "Straight Ahead." You will be in quad number 4. Your quad mates are already checked in and will be part of your therapy group. This is a safe, loving place. We just want to help you become the man God always intended you to be."

"Uh, okay," I said. "So, I have three roommates?"

"Well they are in your quad, but you each have your own room. Obviously, we don't have shared sleeping arrangements here."

I chuckled. "Yeah, guess that would kind of defeat the purpose."

Mormon man grinned a wide plastic smile. "Lead us not into temptation," he remarked. I couldn't help but feel he was giving me an intense overview. His hands touched mine several times as I filled out papers. I swear, it almost looked like he had a boner pressing on his tight polyester grey slacks.

"Um, how long have you worked here," I asked the straight-laced front desk attendant.

"About two years. I am a graduate as well." He stuck his hand out again, "Kevin. Ex-homosexual now happily dating a great girl."

I smiled and returned the handshake. His hand was warm and soft. He held on to my hand quite a long time and extended his hand to grip my shoulder in a benevolent gesture. I got a better glance at his crotch. He was boned up to the max. I could easily make out the mushroom head of his circumcised penis. *Hmm, wonder just how cured he is?*

"I was so sure I could never change the way I thought and felt. But I am a real success story. I am proof you can live a life as a straight man, get turned on by girls, and even perform sexually with a female."

"You've fucked a girl?"

Kevin blushed at my vulgar question, but smiled and nodded. "I have intercourse with my girlfriend all the time."

"Um, isn't that like breaking the godly rules? I thought you weren't supposed to fornicate before you got married?"

"Technically that's true. But one of the perks of this therapy is a permission to have as much intercourse with females as you desire until your body and mind reprograms itself," he said in his most Stepford voice.

"That's interesting," I said. *If straight guys knew about this, they could come here, pretend to like dick, and then start a campaign of bedding every girl they could find and get pats on the back for fucking,* I thought. "Okay, it was nice to meet you, Kevin. Maybe we can talk again soon. I guess I'll go find my room."

"You can come talk any time you like. It really helps to have guys to chat with who know what you are feeling and what you are wanting. I would love to spend a long time chatting with you."

I smiled and turned to leave still with the distinct impression that Kevin would enjoy chatting to me with no pants on even more. I drove out of the lobby area and found Quad 4 easily enough. The grounds of the facility were nice in that high desert sort of way. I could tell the building was going to have a spectacular view of the Three Sisters. I parked and grabbed one of my bags and walked up the sidewalk to Quad 4 and tentatively turned the door handle and walked in.

The room was fairly large with a far wall of windows facing me looking out onto the mountain range. There was a squashy older small sectional couch facing a fireplace and television. Three men sat on the couch watching a baseball game. They turned their heads in unison, each smiling as they saw me come in. The red-headed muscled stocky guy on the end got up and came over to greet me, hand extended.

"Hi. Welcome to Quad 4, Queer Boy central," the young man said, blue eyes twinkling. "I'm Sean. This is JaMarcus," Sean said pointing to the large black guy in the middle of the couch. He stuck out his hand which engulfed my own.

"Welcome to the jungle, brother," he said with a big grin. This here is Manuel, Manny to all of us." A smallish Latino man extended his hand. He was probably in his mid to late thirties. He was dark and handsome, with a sweet energy and a killer smile. A dark goatee framed his full lips. I felt my dick actually begin to swell and I tried to think of anything else.

"¿Que paso, hermano?" he said coming over and actually giving me a big hug. The other two made their way over and hugged me as well. JaMarcus's hand patted me on the butt several times. This was definitely not what I expected.

"Hi. Thanks for the great welcome. I was worried I was going to be rooming with a bunch of uptight dicks."

"No man, plenty of dicks here but not uptight. Just part of the chain gang with you. So who made you sign up to "Just Say No to Cock?" Sean said taking my duffle bag and laying it on the floor beside the couch, scooting over so I could join the gang.

"Um, my mom mostly. Dad is just going along with her I think."

"So how did she find out you like sucking dong?" JaMarcus asked.

I looked around at these guys and decided then and there it was a safe place. I sighed. "She walked in on me when I was balls deep inside my boyfriend. She screamed and threw a laundry basket full of socks and underwear at my head." The three guys exploded in laughter.

"Classic," Sean said. "That may be the best one yet."

"What about all of you?" I asked clearly interested and now more relaxed than I dreamed I would be.

Sean spoke first. "Not that different than you. My dad had seen a bunch of gay porn stuff in the computer memory cache. He came home early one day when I was sitting naked in front the computer jerking off. Right as I shot my nut up onto my chest and face, he moved around in front of me. I almost shit myself. The interrogation commenced and soon I was admitting to sucking off a couple of friends and letting them fuck me. That was it for him. Hasta la vista, off to "Straight Ahead." The guys murmured with an understanding grunt. We all knew just how that would feel.

"What about you, JaMarcus?"

"Man, it was so fucked up. My church youth group leader had been fucking around with me for a while. I was down with it, you know what I mean? But my mom came home early one day and found us in a big ole 69 and she went and grabbed a shotgun and blew a hole in my bedroom wall aiming for his head."

"Oh my God!" I said in horror while cracking up.

"Yeah, she chased him down the street. He ended up getting arrested and all that shit. It was bad. I mean, I guess he deserved to get arrested and all that, but it fucked me up bad and she blames him on turning me gay and all that."

"You think that's what happened?"

"Unlikely, since I was sucking my cousin's dick when I was about eleven. I just always like boy dick and started wanting it as soon as I was growing hair on my nut, you feel me?"

"I feel you," I said reaching out and fist bumping him. "That's crazy harsh, bro. I'm almost afraid to ask, Manny. But what brought you here?"

"My story might not be as dramatic as you boys, but it's just as messed up. I am a married guy. Have been for ten years. I fooled around with other boys growing up at the same time I also dated and made out with girls and all that. Fell in love and got married. Had a couple of kids. But I been secretly fucking around with guys most of the time. My wife found out on some emails I had sent to guys I was hooking up with. She basically told me I had to come here or she was leaving me. So, here I am."

"Damn, that is super heavy duty, buddy. You think you can kick your taste for dick?"

"Well. I guess I'm gonna try. Not sure if I really believe you can just quit liking it, you know. Maybe you can just decide never to play around again. It's crazy, you know. I like fucking my wife a lot. I just get turned on by cock too."

"So, doesn't that just mean you're bisexual?"

"Yeah, I guess. But she ain't okay with me being a bi." We all laughed.

"What a sorry sack of shit you are," Sean said reaching over and grabbing Manny who jumped up and grabbed him and the two started wrestling and fake punching one another until they lay on the floor in a sweaty heap. I noticed both their dicks were rock hard in their sweatpants.

"Dude, that is so gay," JaMarcus laughed. "We can see your boners all the way over here. You gonna get put in the chair if you don't watch it."

My head snapped around. "Chair? What the fuck is the Chair?"

Sean pulled his shirt off and wiped off his face and back. His chest was big and furry, covered with tiny red fur that disappeared into this sweats. His cock was pointing straight out. Manny took his shirt off and laid back on the carpet. His thick black pits glistening with sweat. His belly was firm and a thick line of black fur ran up the middle of his belly down to his large dick and balls that were clearly outlined in the thin grey sweats.

"The chair is one of the behavior modification therapies they do here if you get caught fooling around with another one of the brothers."

"Does that happen much?"

They all laughed and JaMarcus said, "What do you think? Shit, a lot of guys here ain't ever even sucked a dick until they get sent here and talk about they feelings and get all cozy with guys night and day. Pretty hard not to hook up and get your nut off with a brother. But damn, if you get caught…"

"What do they do? What is this fucking chair?"

"You get strapped into the chair, naked…all spread eagled and shit. They put a probe up your asshole and wrap these electrodes around your cock and balls. Then they show you gay shit and zap you with a painful shock. Then they show you pussy and turn up the good zaps until you have to cum. They do it for hours and hours until you are like going crazy."

"Holy shit. Have any of you?"

"Nah, not yet. We been trying hard to play by the rules. Though these two fools here are fucking around like this all the time, making my dick so hard all I can think about is boning they ass."

Sean and Manny leaned against one another, chests heaving, sweaty and out of breath. Sean draped his large heavy arm around Manny's neck and rubbed the man's furry chest back and forth. This did not strike me as manly behavior, however. *But then, maybe that's what's wrong with me,* I thought. Watching these two be so brotherly together, I began to think…shit, I can do this. I watched Manny spread his legs wide apart, his thick penis sliding down the leg of his sweats. My own dick began to harden as I watched him slide his hand up and down his shaft.

"Yo, Amigo. I am gonna have to go rub one off if you keep that up," Manny joked. "I hope they picked a better porno for today."

I laughed and looked puzzled which caused the guys to join in with the laughs. Manny spoke. "Every day, they put another porno DVD in the player. If you get the urge to make out with a guy or fantasize about dick, you are supposed to go watch the DVD and jack off to straight porn."

I thought about this. I had seen plenty of straight porn and had gotten myself off plenty while watching it. I had a feeling these guys knew about my trick. "So is this regular porn, like a guy and girl fucking, or what?"

"If we are lucky, yeah. But sometimes these putas just give us girl on girl porn, just watch these cunts with the long nails pulling their nasty pussy apart and eating one another out. Damn, I don't know what the guys get out of that at all. As long as it's a guy banging some bitch, then you can always just watch the dick, you know homes?"

I smiled. "That was always what I did with my straight friends when they wanted to look at porn. I could get as hard as anybody. Just watched the dicks."

"Yeah, we figure they will only let us do that so much before making us watch the vagina monologues again," Sean said. He stood up and stretched; his penis hard and rigid against his sweats. I stared at it and felt myself grow even harder. Manny reached over and gripped his dick.

"Man, you gotta put that away. You are killing me, hermano."

There was a knock at the door and the guys' demeanors changed from frivolous to serious in one second. JaMarcus hopped up and opened the door. A wide-grinning man came in. He was probably in his early thirties. He wore a pair of navy slacks and a short-sleeved white polo shirt. He was in good shape and his muscles threatened to pop the seams on the sleeves. Without trying, I also noticed a full rounded bulge in his pants that moved from side to side as he walked into the room. He stretched out his hand to me and grinned even wider.

"You must be Dylan. So glad to see you, brother. I'm Saul Winters. I'll be your group leader and counselor. We will be spending a lot of time together. I know the guys will fill you in on most of the day-to-day expectations. I will come by later today and go over some specifics and do your initial intake screening." Saul turned the rest of the guys. "Time to head over to the gym, fellows. Team sports and athletics. See you all there. Get ready to work up a sweat and get your manly motors roaring." With that, Saul waved and left the apartment. I looked around at the guys who were just staring at one another.

"Is he for real?" I asked.

"Oh yeah. Time to get sweaty with the other boys. Guideline #1 – Participate in sports activities to maximize straight masculine relationships." JaMarcus rattled off from memory. There's a whole wall of rules like that we get to learn.

"But...plenty of gay guys are athletic and do sports together all the time. I mean, some of them probably do sports because they get to be physical and close with other guys," I said.

"Not to mention shower time..." Sean said with a sly grin.

"Or time on the training table having a rubdown or some therapy," Manny said with a wistful look in his eyes.

I shook my head. "Playing shirts and skins basketball is not going to make me want to date a girl," I said matter of factly.

JaMarcus slung his big arm around my neck. "Now you getting it, brother."

Thirty minutes later, I was shirtless and sweating as I held my own on a volleyball team made up of guys from around the center. The guys were all shapes and sizes, some of them clearly good at sports, others were flabby and older. Some were effeminate, others were very masculine. Some graceful, others were clumsy. I got into the game. It had been a while since I had done much physical activity other than marching band and it felt good to move my body. I wore these gym shorts that were fairly tight. They hugged my ass and had a nice pouch that allowed my junk to bounce and move with my body. I hadn't bothered with a jock and my underwear didn't hold in my boys very well. I watched several of the team stare at me. As I bent over to take a breather, I could feel them starring at my ass. When I served the ball, I watched them out of the corner of my eye look at my armpits and chest and follow the trickle of sweat from my chest down my belly into my shorts. Jumping around on the gym floor, I could feel all eyes follow the bouncing balls. I wasn't the only one either. To my right, a monstrously tall man, probably 6-6, with a big belly, sported tight fitting sweats and his sausage was poking out and his bull balls were hanging low. He managed to fondle himself about every thirty seconds. He didn't have his shirt off, but his t-shirt was stuck to his furry chest and left nothing to the imagination.

On the other end of the gym, a game of basketball was in full swing. Sweaty, shirtless men rubbed against each other and fought for the ball. I didn't think I had ever seen a game played so closed and physical. JaMarcus's arms flew around a tall blond guy defending him. Their chests were practically touching. I saw man hands on hips and butts and bellies. If this was supposed to make me forget about sucking dicks and start wanting a mouthful of pussy, I just wasn't following it. But, *what the fuck,* I thought. *I can at least enjoy the exercise and manly camaraderie.* I watched Brother Saul playing hard with the basketball boys. His muscles were amazingly defined. His smooth skin was flawless, big dark quarter sized nipples shone with sweat. His chestnut treasure trail of belly fur disappeared into his sweaty shorts. I could see the clear outline of his circumcised penis press against the thin fabric of his shorts. There was no doubt to me, this was a man's man for sure. And I wanted him to fuck me senseless. From the way others were staring, I wasn't the only one at all.

After two hours of sports and manly bonding, it was time to hit the showers. I was frankly shocked that a bunch of cock gobblers like us were being allowed and expected to participate in group open showers. But as we were heading into the locker room, I felt a big arm slide around my shoulders. It was Saul. He smelled damp and sour, sweaty and musky. I practically shot my nut in my shorts as I breathed in his smell.

"I saw you looking a little confused there, brother. Don't worry. We try to put you in normal situations that all masculine men participate in. It's good to enjoy the brotherhood and team spirit of sports and locker rooms. We just try and help you understand and participate in them like a typical heterosexual man. So, just relax and enjoy bonding with one another. No shame or fear in being naked with other men. And I will be in there to make sure no one forgets the rules and starts to slip into bad habits."

I stared at him, soaking in the sweat and heat of his body. He pulled my head to his lips and actually planted a kiss on the side of my head. "So glad you are here, little bro. You are going to do great. You will be dreaming of pussy before you know it."

I grinned and actually leaned in closer to him as we walked. Strangely enough, pussy was not remotely on my mind. "I'm feeling a bit uncomfortable so is it okay if I shower near you?"

"You bet, little buddy," Saul said. "Stick with me and I will show you the ropes. Go get your gear and bring it back to this locker," he said pointing to the one beside him. I literally ran to the locker I had stashed my gear in and was back just in time to watch Saul bend over and slide his sweat soaked shorts down to the floor. His dingy Bike jock gripped his meaty ass, thick brown hair running down the crack. As he bent down, I caught a glimpse of the full pouch trying in vain to corral his manly scrotum. Breathless, I put down my things and slid off my shorts forgetting I didn't have a jock on. My dick stuck out in a semi-hard pose that seemed shocking and obvious. He turned around and gently smiled.

"Nice woody, little bro. Grab your towel and come with me," Saul said sliding his jock down his thick legs to lie in a pool on the floor. It took all my strength not to pick it up and slide it over my head. I grabbed a towel and wrapped it around my waist, following his naked ass into the showers.

The shower room was already hot and thick with steam. Saul pulled up at a shower pole and turned the handle, jets of water blasting on his big chest. He pumped some shower soap into his palm and began to wash his pits. I stood beside him and did the same. My penis was now almost fully erect. I looked around the shower room, most everyone else had a boner like me. I noticed that Saul's dick was almost as hard as mine. He seemed content to let it bob and flop, so I did the same. I wanted him to wash me, to grip my cock and slide a soapy finger deep inside my ass. But he just did the rub a dub beside me instead, making my balls turn bluer by the minute.

"It's great, isn't it? Bathing with brothers like this. See, you don't need to have sexual relations with a brother to enjoy being naked and free with them."

I wondered if Saul was just legitimately obtuse about how hard and provocative this was for most of us, or if he really did think that by immersing us in all this manly stew of nakedness and forbidding us to act on our clearly natural impulses, that we somehow would lose those feelings. It made about as much sense as taking a fat guy to a buffet and telling him to just enjoy the smells and think he would not be interested in filling up his plate again and again. When we left the showers, Saul draped a hand around my shoulders and pulled me close to talk privately.

"I know this is hard for you. It's hard for me too. Part of me still wants to bend you over and fuck your boy hole until I blast my nut in your cunt. But you will feel the change soon enough and once you get better at pussy, you will forget more about the dick. After we get dressed, let's have our intake meeting."

I nodded, more turned on and blinded by my lust than ever. I noticed Saul's penis had a long, clear string of precum dangling from the tip. He might be all about the puss now, but I don't think his dick had gotten the message. We dressed and tossed our towels in the pile with the other wet things and I followed Saul to his office. Sean and JaMarcus waved and gave me a funny thumbs-up.

Chapter 3
Reprogramming for Dummies

Saul ushered me into his office and closed the door. It was comfortable, if small, and had a cozy love seat across from his desk. He invited me to sit down and he went behind his desk.

"Again, Dylan. We are so glad you are here. We are committed to find ways to make you a normal heterosexual male. It is just a matter of changing the track that your train is on. For some reason, your train got derailed off the mainline and is taking an alternate route. But you can switch it back and get back on the right track to take you to pussy town, which is where all red-blooded guys like us ultimately want to go."

I smiled. "Actually, I don't want to go to pussy town. I would rather go to Penis Town if that's all the same to you. I don't feel broken or off track. I am just heading to a different town than other guys. It doesn't make my town any worse."

Saul grinned. "I've sure been there, myself. But trust me, once you experience the true joys of opposite-sex sexual intercourse, you will see you were shortchanging yourself before."

I just shrugged. I highly doubted any of this but I still was determined to try. If they could rewire me, it would be easier to be straight. But it sure didn't seem to make much sense to me. Saul was leaned back in his chair. His legs were spread wide apart and the bulge in his trousers was still highly distracting to me. I stared at the outline of his penis and felt my own grow a bit bigger.

"So, I am going to do an intake interview with you. Some of the questions will just be ordinary family history. But others are going to be a bit intimate, a bit confrontational. I need you to be totally honest and try to tell me everything. It will help us chart the best path to recovery for you. After the interview, I will be conducting a penile plethysmograph test. Do you know what that is?"

I shook my head, thinking about the "chair" device the guys back in my quad referred to. I swallowed and felt my palms begin to sweat.

"I know it sounds scary. But it's not, I promise. Here is the device," he held up a small loop of plastic covered coiled wire. It looked fragile and delicate. "We measure your penis and find the right size loop. Then you slide it on your penis just up behind the head. Then I show you some photos and you listen to some stories read to you, and we measure what makes you get an erection. That way, we know if you have some latent hetero tendencies that just need to be turned on or if you really just like guys only and have to start over leaning how to have sex the right way."

This sounded crazy to me but I just shook my head like I understood and agreed with this crazy-ass gobbley-gook. Saul began the questioning about my family, siblings, church affiliation, schooling, yada-yada. I was only half-assed participating, mostly watching his fat crotch move and roll in his thin slacks.

"When did you first experiment with another boy with sex?"

"Huh?"

Saul repeated the question, adjusting his big balls as he did. I swallowed.

"Um, I was like ten or so."

"Who did you experiment with?"

"My older friend."

"Just like me," Saul said with a nod of his head. "What did you boys do together?"

"Not much. He taught me how to jerk off. He showed me his dick and had me stroke it. Shot some of his nut into my mouth. Showed me how to put on a condom."

"Did he anally penetrate you?"

"What? Eww, no. He probably would have liked that but he didn't fuck me."

"What about you and your boyfriend?"

"Barely. We had only just started trying everything. But yeah, he penetrated me. I fucked him too."

"Did you ejaculate in each other's mouths?"

I just stared. "Yes." I watched Saul's penis flex and press against his pants. "It's pretty great, you know."

Saul smiled. "I did that plenty and bent over for a man to anally enter me many times as well. But now I know I like pussy more," he said in a less than definitive tone.

"But shooting your wad in a guy's mouth or ass is pretty great too, right?" I said.

Saul looked conflicted and just shook his head and rubbed his dick again. He flipped his pad to some other questions and continued. "How often do you masturbate?"

"As much as I can," I said proudly.

"Good. We want you to cum as much as you can. We just need you to fantasize about women while you do so."

"Yeah, that's not really what gets my dick hard," I said shrugging.

"Don't worry. It will soon enough. Okay, that's enough questions for now. Let's measure your penis and start the other exam. Can you take off your pants and shorts and come around here so I can measure you?"

I robotically stood and slid my pants down thinking, this has got to be the gayest thing anyone has ever asked me to do…at anti-gay camp, nonetheless. I pushed down my underwear and walked around the desk. My cock was sticking straight out, a drop of precum on the tiny lips. Saul reached out and gripped my penis and casually slid his thumb over the juice and rubbed it into the head of my dick.

"I always have tons of precum too," he said spending way too much time rubbing my penis lips until even more fluid flowed out. He reached over and took one of the wire looped coils and carefully rolled it onto my shaft just behind my glans. "That one's a little too big I think," he said. He rolled it off and selected the next smallest size. It rolled on and snuggly fit against my dick, right behind the flare of my penis head. "That one seems just right. Okay, some over here and sit in this recliner." Saul took me by the hand and had me walk into a small closet sized room with a big chair. I got even harder thinking about all the men and boys how had sat bareass naked in this chair with their dick wired up to some stupid machine. Saul took some electrode wires and connected them to the dainty coil. He moved my dick and balls with his hands until he had them softly laying on the top of my legs. His hands eased my boys around in the sack, tenderly adjusting them. There was a screen in front of me and headphones on the back of the chair. He took the headphones. "Put these on. You will see images and hear some descriptive stories. Just lay back and let your penis do what it wants to do. If you get hard, great. If not, great. You will also see a red light appear on the screen. You need to click this button when you see it. This is so you don't sit here and close your eyes. You need to click the button every time you see the red light. If you shoot your nut while we are doing the test, just let it shoot and I'll help you clean up later. Okay, you understand?" Saul's hand gently stroked my deflating penis and the pubes surrounding my junk. I nodded my head. He smiled and closed the door. The darkness enveloped me. Part of me wondered if some shock was going to zap my dick every time I got hard looking at some guy fucking another guy. My heart was beating so fast.

"Okay, starting now. Just relax and let your dick do what it wants to do," he said through the speakers in my headphones.

The first image was of fields and flowers, then forest animals. Soft music played. A flipping rainbow photo, then clouds, then little ducks, then boom…a big breasted woman with her legs spread wide, a furry vagina gaping open. My penis retreated within like a frightened turtle. More vaginas now, close ups. Those ones with the wet red insides and frilly skin that poured out like a wet box of Kleenex. I shuddered and closed my eyes for a moment then opened them again. This time, there was a very young girl on the screen, soft hairless vagina pulled apart with her small fingers. The red light appeared just above her vulva. I clicked the button and closed my eyes. These photos seemed like child porn to me. It was horrible. My dick was practically internal genitalia by this time.

Suddenly, the screen filled with a big mustached man with a furry chest and an erect eight-inch penis. I was suddenly much more interested. I watched the man casually stroke his penis and milk a drop of precum from the large head. His legs were spread wide and his heavy sack rested on the cushion of the chair he was sitting in. My dick responded and swelled, tightening around the loop circling my shaft. I smiled imagining how the sensor graphs were looking to Saul. It took all my concentration to not start jacking off. I was desperate to cum. I suddenly noticed the red light and wondered how long it had been on. I clicked the button about ten times in a row until it went off. The next slide loaded. Two athletic jock types were in a deep sixty-nine together, swallowing one another's penis with hungry abandon. The red light appeared right on the nutsack of one of the boys and I clicked. Then it appeared on the sack of the other one. I clicked. Then it appeared on the asshole of one of the boys. I clicked again. The next slide came on. This one showed a young man with his mouth open, another man ejaculating a huge creamy load on his tongue and face. The red light appeared on the boy's mouth, and I clicked. Then it appeared on the shaft of the ejaculating penis. I clicked again.

The next slide loaded and it was a young girl, disturbingly young again to me. She was sitting in the lap of some old guy with his thick cock crammed up inside her tight vagina. Her face looked pained and uncomfortable. I saw the red light appear on her pussy and I clicked. This photo was making me mad. I didn't want to see any of this. More photos of guys fucking women with big tits. Lots of close ups of cocks sliding inside big furry pussies or up some woman's ass filled the screen. I clicked away but my dick stayed limp. Next a photo of a young boy in the shower came on, his small hairless dick was erect and he was grinning like an idiot. The red light bounced on his small penis and I clicked, dismayed that my penis stirred a bit. The next slide was of two young men being fondled by a dad. My dick got even harder. I wanted to close my eyes but that damn red light kept me looking. The next slide showed a young boy on his back, his legs spread wide. A dad's cock was stuffed up his butt. His eyes were closed and he was almost sucking on a finger. Now this was making me real mad. I decided I couldn't stay quiet any more.

"Why are you showing me this shit? I would never look at crap like this. How is this helping you? Aren't these photos illegal?"

Saul's voice came over the headphones I was wearing. "It's just to see how you react to different stimuli. The photos came from law enforcement. It's an older set they used to use when giving this evaluation. We have permission to use the images."

"What kind of test are you talking about?"

There was no response for a long time. The images kept shifting between younger girls and younger boys getting fucked or sucking on dicks. Finally Saul spoke. "They use these for treating sex offenders."

The words hit me like a ton of bricks. My mouth went dry and my pulse sped up. Suddenly, the headphones were filled with a recorded voice of a man reading some story. I listened, angry and shaking.

"The boy came into your room while you were drying off from your shower. He was wearing a towel. You smiled and asked him to take the towel off. He grinned and let it drop to the ground. His penis was hard and dripping with precum. He looked just like the kind of boy you love. You wanted to sink to your knees so you could suck him. This is the kind of boy you dream of and you want to fuck him now…" The story continued like this for some time. My cock was hard as a rock again, part from the slutty story and part from anger. I ripped the headphones off my head.

"Okay. I'm done. I am not going to listen to any more of this shit or look at any more kids having sex. This is so fucked up I don't even know what to say." I pulled the electrodes off the loop and rolled it off my boner. I stood up and opened the door of the small room and winced as the bright light hit my eyes. I saw in horror that Saul wasn't the only person in the room. Some other man, older and balding was watching the monitors along with Saul. I suddenly realized I didn't have my pants on and my dick was still hard. I involuntarily covered up my genitals. I noticed the strange man had a lump in his own pants and a darkening spot where his penis was pressing against the tan fabric.

"Um. I need my pants," I said with less ferocity than I felt before. Saul came around the desk and handed me my pants and underwear. The other man casually adjusted his crotch and left the room. Saul's face was pained and his eyes almost looked like they were watering.

"Here, buddy. I'm sorry about that. I don't like that test thing either. You did fine. No need to do that again." Saul's arms came around me and I stepped toward him. My dick pressed against his belly. I felt his hands rub my back and then down to my bare backside. He slowly caressed my ass as his face rubbed against mine. He placed a tender kiss on the side of my face and then stepped back, holding me at arm's length.

"Please don't think that was my idea, Dylan."

I stared at him trying to figure this guy out. "Maybe not, but it was a shitty thing to have to sit through."

"I know. I've been trying to get them to abandon it and not use it any more. But the director thinks the data will help in your recovery."

"How in the hell should it? Big surprise, my dick didn't move for the pussy and got hard with the dicks. And what the fuck is going on with making me watch the kids? I don't want to fuck some young boy or girl and it doesn't mean anything if my dick responds to that shit because I don't look at crap like that." I stepped into my underwear and then my pants. My chest was heaving, I was so mad.

"I know. Try to just forget all about it. Believe it or not, some guys do get hard looking at the nude women even if they have never seen them before. For some of them, that's a breakthrough."

"Well it's not for me. Those pussies just give me the creeps. I am glad other guys love girls and want to fuck them. It's just not for me."

"Maybe you just need some practice," Saul said with a tender voice.

I stared at him. "I would rather practice sucking your dick," I said reaching my hand between his legs and feeling his warm erection against my palm. His eyes closed and he moved to grip my hand, but instead, spread his legs wider apart. I massaged his penis and balls. I could feel his warm breath on my face. I slid my hand into his pants and fumbled with his underwear until I was holding his pulsing cock.

"I can't…" Saul said in a weak protest. "Even if I wanted to, I just can't."

"But your dick says you can," I whispered into his ear.

Saul's hand closed on my penis and rubbed it through my pants. Our faces were so close. I could feel my hand wet from his precum. Our lips slightly closed on each other's. Then he broke away, pushing my hand from his pants.

"No. It's normal for us to get tempted but we can't give into those desires. I need to go sleep with my girlfriend and have an orgasm with her."

I looked at him in stunned silence. I turned to leave but turned back and said. "You do that. But the whole time your dick is inside her, you're gonna be wishing it was inside me."

Chapter 4
The Eleven Steps to Pray the Gay Away

I was still shaking when I made my way back to my quad. When I opened the door, I couldn't see anything except the television on. I figured my roommates were in their bedrooms. I grabbed my duffle bags and headed toward the side of the quad where the sleeping quarters were. As I turned into the hall and looked back at the living room, I saw Sean and Manny lying on the couch, trying to melt into the darkness. Their pants were down around their ankles, their hard dicks were wet and shining in the flicker of the television. I stared at them and finally Sean gave me a small wave.

"Busted," he whispered.

"Don't tell, amigo," Manny said sitting up, worry written on his face.

I just shook my head and went to the empty room I saw down the hall and closed the door. For some reason, seeing Sean with Manny made me even more upset. *What the hell was that about,* I wondered? I took a look around. The room was small and very sterile. I put my clothes away in the drawers. I took the folded sheets on the foot of my bed and put them on the mattress and tucked in the blanket. I pulled off my clothes and grabbed a towel and headed to the bathroom. I had taken a shower just a short while ago but I felt dirty and didn't know what else to do. I walked naked down the hallway, feeling the stares of Sean and Manny on my bare ass. I walked into the bathroom. One of the two showers was running, JaMarcus I figured. I went to the other one and leaned inside and turned on the water. I hung the towel on a hook and turned to get in. My attention was taken by the dark shape inside the other shower. The curtain was partly opened and I saw the brown glistening flesh turn and casually stroke his soaped up cock. It was impressive, more than seven inches. The man was masturbating and had his other hand up inside his ass as he stroked. I could hear his breathing. I found my penis and began to jack it in rhythm with JaMarcus. His eyes were closed. I quietly moved to my shower and slid the curtain halfway closed and I smiled as I heard the slapping and popping sounds of his hand sliding back and forth over his thick cock. I joined the chorus and soon we were both happily smacking our dicks with our hands as we masturbated in the hot soapy water.

"That you, Dylan?" JaMarcus asked breathlessly.

"Yeah," I said breathing hard.

"You ready to bust your nut?"

"Almost there," I said.

"You thinking of pussy?"

"Not really," I said with a laugh. The shower curtain pulled back and JaMarcus stepped in as he continued to slide his hand furiously back and forth on his large cock.

"Me neither," he said. He leaned close and a thick jet of white cum blasted on my cock and then onto my belly and into my pubes. I closed my eyes and felt my own semen blast out, coating JaMarcus's large penis. He massaged the sperm into his skin and jacked his cock some more.

"Damn, white boy. You needed that nut bad, brother, he said. He scooped up a wad of jizz on his finger and slid it inside his mouth. "Fuck, I love the taste of cum. Guess you can tell, we ain't exactly perfect with our abstinence shit with each other. You see those other idiots sucking dick out there when you came in?"

I nodded.

"Yeah, those boys are gonna be in the chair before you know it. How was your intake session?"

"Terrible," I said. I proceeded to tell JaMarcus the whole story as we got out of the water and dried off. We stood naked in the bright bathroom as I told the tale. He smiled and shook his head in understanding.

"Yeah, man. That is some fucked up shit, for sure. We all had to do that. I decided when I saw all that crap to just try and keep my dick hard the whole time. That way, they don't know what shit turns me on."

The door opened and Sean and Manny walked in. They were wearing underwear that did nothing to hide their erections. They listened to the last of the story I was telling and shook their heads.

"Y'all get through blowing one another?" JaMarcus said with a grin.

"No comprende, Homes," Manny said. Sean reached over to give the man a fist-bump.

"Um hum," JaMarcus said. "Y'all gonna be in the chair before you know it."

"Well we won't be alone. Looks like you guys enjoyed some protein of your own." Sean reached over and picked at a fat glob of semen in my pubes. He sniffed and then licked the semen off his finger. "Yep, tastes like JaMarcus for sure."

They all laughed. Sean and Manny pulled off their underwear and got in the showers to rinse off. I watched their balls roll in their full sacks as they bent down to pull off their shorts. Sean kept his shower curtain open, soaping his nuts and deflating boner as he talked with me. His bright red hair was a thick carpet around his penis. Manny's furry ass disappeared into the other shower and I wanted to pull back the curtain and pull his cheeks apart and see just how far I could get my head inside his ass. But I kept looking at Sean. Those eyes of his were like sparkling jewels. Something about the way the corners of his eyes crinkled and the mischievous grin on his face, not to mention the red hair made me weak in the knees. I tried to remember the last time I had really thought about Peter, who was supposed to be my boyfriend and I had the feeling whatever we had was not going to make it through this next phase of my life. The guys got out and dried off and soon we were all in the small kitchenette with JaMarcus making grilled cheese sandwiches wearing an apron and no pants. The rest of us sat around naked, munching on the crunchy toast and laughing at our own experiences with the intake slides.

"I was like, Dios Mio! I have kids about that age and now here I am watching this girl riding the cock of that old perv. And those boys! Shit, made me hard in like two seconds and I never think about shit like that."

I laughed. The absurdity of the whole situation was almost more than I could bear. Here I was naked in a kitchen with three other delectable men, all of whom I would gladly suck or fuck. I knew they felt exactly the same. And the futility of pretending to think otherwise was stunning.

"So, hey. Do any of you really think this program works? Do you really think guys will change? Cause from what I felt and saw with Saul today, I don't care what he says, he is still a cock gobbler."

Sean spit out his beer. "That guy is so fucking hot, it's all I can do to keep my hands off him. I don't know, I guess it might work for some of the guys here."

"Do any of you really want it to work for you?"

"I do," Manny said. But between you and me, I'm always gonna love cock. It's just the way I am wired, you know?"

I nodded. "It's the way all of us are wired and there's nothing fucking wrong with that. And even if I pretend to like girls and even fuck one, I will still be wishing it was your furry ass instead. Speaking of girls, when do we get to hang out with some? This is the gayest thing I have ever done, just sitting around naked with a bunch of queers who just got through sucking on one another." The men all laughed.

"Pretty soon. But we can't hang with girls unless it's all about dating or warm-up shit for going to bed with one of them. Not just palling around with a girl. That's way too gay, they say. Real men don't do that. They hang with other men until they are ready to fornicate," Sean said with a sly grin.

"You gotta learn the Eleven Steps, Homes," Manny said. "Then you will know."

"What the hell..." I said.

JaMarcus reached over and picked up a laminated card off the kitchen counter. "They have them posted everywhere. The leaders here think these are the Eleven Commandments for turning a guy straight."

I looked at the card and read:

The Eleven Steps to Heterosexual Male Success
– Based on the teachings of Joe Nicolosi

1. Participate in contact or team sports activities with men
2. Avoid queer activities such as going to art museums or attending the theater or musicals, opera, or symphonies
3. Avoid women unless for romantic contact
4. Increase time spent with heterosexual men in order to mimic their behavior

5. Attend church and join men's groups
6. Attend reparative therapy group sessions
7. Become assertive with women through flirting and dating
8. Begin heterosexual dating
9. Fuck a woman
10. Get married to a woman
11. Father children

I looked up at my roommates. Each one of them were chewing on their lips to keep from smiling or laughing. "What...the...fuck...?" I said, my eyes wide with wonder.

"You already saw how effective the sports contact is for all these guys. Shit, they all went back to the quad and rubbed one off for sure after all that stimulation. They think rubbing on another man doing sports will get the urge out of you. Might be that way for a straight man, but damn, makes me want to bend all of you over and ride you all night," JaMarcus said.

"They think going to a museum or a play makes you gay," I said. "That's the stupidest thing I've ever heard.

"I know, man. I never do any of that shit and I love sucking cock. My little brother goes to musicals and art museums all the time and he fucks pussy like there's no tomorrow," Manny added.

"And number 3...no messing around with women unless it's on a date where the end result might be you and her getting into bed."

"That's crazy," I said.

"Well, that's what this place is all about," Sean said. "And you're right. If we keep fucking around with one another, we are just going to end up in the chair."

"You know, if the chair is so damn successful in modifying our sinful behavior, it would save a lot of time if they just started with that," I said clearly annoyed.

"Don't give them any ideas, Homes," Manny said. "I hate to say it, but I think all of us end up there before this is all over."

"Sounds like fucking "Clockwork Orange" or something," I said disgusted and oddly enough, turned on. My emotions were like a revolving door these days. Half the time I wanted to kill my parents, the other times, I missed them like crazy and was ready to go home and promise I would never touch another guy. But down deep inside, I just didn't believe that. I missed my friends, especially Peter. We had barely started getting to know each other when we got torn apart. I missed the girls that liked hanging out with me too, the ones who were looking for a fun guy who wouldn't just want to try and fuck them. My posse of girls were fun and happy and we had a blast together. I loved each one of them in my own way and had even fantasized about sleeping with them. Sometimes it would make my dick get hard, other times it didn't.

The girls: Renee, Jennifer, Tara, and Amy hung out with me and Peter and a couple of other guys from band, Karl and Casey. I had a suspicion about them being queer too, I guess you could say my gay-dar pinged pretty loudly when they were around. But so far, neither had made a move and I had never seen them in any compromising position, unlike Kyle and Robby had displayed on the back of the bus.

The gang of girls would sit with us in the lunchroom and talk about movies, politics, music, or gossip about people. They treated us like princes, doting on us, making as much body contact with us as you could without actually making out. I was constantly being touched, my hair played with, and a hand on my thigh or arms around me. The girls loved being able to be affectionate without having to worry that we would expect them to put out. Sometimes, we would hold hands or walk down the hall arm in arm, but it was never much of a sexual turn-on to me.

Twice, I had gone further with one of the girls. I laid on my bed with Renee once and let her slide her hand inside my pants and shorts, fondling my penis until I grew hard. She told me she had never seen a dick and I pulled it out and let her explore to her heart's content. Eventually, she slid my cock in her mouth and sucked me until I came. She was fascinated with the hard softness of it, the silky pubes that framed my junk, my big balls, and the pearly white semen that splashed on my furry belly as she pulled away and watched my orgasm.

It had been pretty much the same with Tara. But with her, I was at her house and she asked if I would get naked and lay on the bed with her. I had shrugged my shoulders and nodded and pulled off my clothes, feeling more awkward and naked than when I was in the showers after gym class. She pulled her clothes off. Her small breasts were perky and pink and I did want to touch them. She took my hand and laid it on the small warm mounds. I felt my dick swell, more from the excitement of the situation than from touching her. Her hands found my dick and she softly stroked it and touched me. She took my hand and put it on her vulva. I didn't know what I was doing. She tried to get me interested in playing with something up inside there, but I just laughed and pulled my hand away. It was so wet and slick, but it felt utterly foreign.

And that had been it for my heterosexual experimentation. I had to admit, it had been curious and somewhat pleasurable. But for the most part, it felt like I was someone else, not myself. It did not compare to the trembling intensity of what Peter and I had discovered together. I knew that Manny obviously knew all about sex with girls. I wondered about the other guys.

"So Sean. Did you ever try on some pussy for size?" I asked.

Sean laughed. "Yeah. I mean, I went out with quite a few girls. I liked their company and all that. Got hand jobs from three of them. I even did my best to flick their bean to help them get off, though I didn't know what the hell I was doing. Last year, I dated a girl for quite a while. She was awesome, had a great time with her. We had a lot in common. She would suck me off which was nice but also a little weird cause I didn't always get hard.

Finally, one night after she had been hinting for a long time, I went ahead and fucked her. It was okay. When we were doing it missionary style, I was really distracted and not enjoying it that much. Then I flipped her over and started fucking her from the back, while I totally imagined I was boning her little brother and dad. And *voila*, I was a fucking machine. But after a few weeks of that, she started asking why I always liked to do it from the back. When I didn't have a good answer, she just straight up asked if I was gay. Was the first time I actually came out and said it. She was actually pretty cool about it and was glad I told her. Not long after that was when my dad walked in on my stroking to porn. I think he was pretty miffed that I stopped seeing Cara."

"Damn," I said in a quiet voice. "What about you JaMarcus?"

"Nah, man. I never fucked around with a girl. My mom was okay with it 'cause she was real big on no sex before marriage. Shit, I have no idea what she thought I was doing hanging out with the youth group leader all the time. My brother knew I was banging him. He teased me about not liking pussy all the time. I had plenty of girls hit on me, some even tried to jack me or asked to suck me. I'd just be polite and say no, I'm saving it for marriage. Most of the time, they were down with that. But you know they was wanting to unwrap the sausage."

The guys laughed. I looked at Manny. "Did you just grow up wanting girls only?"

He grinned his big toothy smile. "Ah, you know. I played around with boys and all that a bit when I was growing up. Got my ass cherry popped when I was young out in a barn with other boys. We just did that kind of shit. I fucked a girl for the first time when I was sixteen. It was great. I just sort of kept playing with boys on the side too, though. I love fucking my wife, you know? I'm not turned on by pussy in general. Just hers cause I love her and everything. But most of the time, I was fucking around with college boys and coworkers and my boss and everyone else."

"So how many guys do you think you've been with, Romeo?" Sean asked.

Manny thought for a while. "Not sure. Quite a few."

"Guess," Sean said.

"Couple of hundred probably in the past 15 years or so."

"Holy shit, you are a man-whore for sure," JaMarcus said. We all laughed.

The intercom button squawked and a voice came over the speaker. "Good evening, gentlemen. We hope you had a great, straight-thinking day. Remember, tomorrow is male mentor day. We will get started around 10:00. Make the most of your bonding and heterosexual intimate time with your mentor. He can make a real difference in your development toward being the straight man God created you to be. Sweet dreams, fellows."

I looked at the group. "What the fuck?"

Manny explained. "Oh yeah, homes. Tomorrow, these older dudes take us out to do manly shit and hope their straight mojo rubs off on us to make us ready to hump girls."

I laughed. "That is the stupidest thing I ever heard."

Sean agreed. "You know, it's pretty cool hanging out with the dads though. Last time, mine took me golfing, he paid for everything.

And at the end, got to take a shower with him in the clubhouse. His dick was harder than mine."

"See! This is crazy. Hanging out with some macho dad is going to be a huge turn on to me too. Don't they get that?"

"Clearly not," Sean said. "Just enjoy it, brother."

I shrugged my shoulders. "I guess I will."

Chapter 5
The Benevolent Brotherhood of Man

The four of us headed to the cafeteria for breakfast along with guys from the other quads. Looking around, it seemed like most of the quads were a collection of guys about like ours: young guys, married guys, different ethnicities, and a few dads. Everyone looked a bit shell-shocked to me, with many not wanting to make much eye contact. I chatted with my quad mates and wondered what this next crazy adventure was going to be like. I excused myself to go take a leak. I walked into the bathroom to see one of the dad types standing at the other urinal. I pulled up beside him and looked over and smiled, nodding my head to say good morning. There weren't any privacy panels between the toilets (another thing that was more tempting in this place that was supposed to cure me.)

"How's it going?" I said with a smile. My right arm was actually touching the guy's arm. *This is really tight quarters for a pisser,* I thought.

"Pretty good. I'm Doug," he said almost reaching over to shake my hand when we both laughed. He seemed to relax and it appeared he actually took a small step back from the urinal. Before, he was practically climbing inside the thing. I glanced down and caught a glimpse of a thick round dick head and a big set of daddy balls covered with fur. I moved my hand to the other side for some reason to give him a clear view of my own junk. He stared and slowly manipulated his penis until it began to grow hard. I did the same, feeling my arm rub against his.

"Man, you have a great dick," he whispered looking around to see if anyone was in the bathroom.

"So do you, Dad," I said with a grin. "You like looking at boys like me?"

"Guess that's why I'm here. What about you?"

"Same. Never fucked with a dad but I think it would be fun."

"You have no idea," Doug whispered. I watched as his fist pumped quickly back and forth on his cock. I did the same. We turned to one another and in a soft chorus of grunts, we shot our nut on one another's penis. Doug lifted a string of my semen to his lips and tasted. I did the same.

"Thanks," he said reaching over and rubbing my neck. He leaned close and kissed me on the side of my mouth. "I'm in Quad 6 if you ever want to talk or anything."

"Thanks, Doug. I'll see you around I'm sure." Doug flushed and gave my ass a fatherly pat as he turned to leave. I waited a few moments and followed him out just as two other guys stumbled into the bathroom. As I left, I heard one of them say. "Does it sorta smell like jizz in here to you?" I walked faster back to the table.

"Did you fall in, Dylan? Damn, you must have had some good butt sex in there to take that long," Sean whispered into my ear. I just smiled. "Fuck me, you did fool around in there, didn't you..?"

"I don't know what you are talking about."

Saul was at the front of the dining hall and spoke into a microphone. "Good morning, men. I hope all of you had a great night. This will be a tremendous day. We have some impressive guests with us today. The men you see up here at the front table are all retire military men from the area. Most are affiliated with local men's groups at churches. This will be a wonderful day of male bonding and sharing. These are real men, men's men who love God and love women. They are committed to helping each of you attain the heterosexual masculinity that you were created to have. We will be pairing you up with these men. Listen up and come forward when we call your name."

I felt my pulse actually quicken as this funny auction began, wondering who the poor sap was that was going to get saddled with me. I was pretty sure I wasn't going to fill them with confidence that I was going to be a straight shooter by the end of the day. Manny's name was called and he went up and shook hands with a gigantic black man with bulging muscles. *Glad that wasn't my partner,* I thought. JaMarcus was called up to partner with a much smaller man, a thick Asian guy with a goatee and glasses. That would be interesting, I figured. Sean was called up and grinned as a big, burly red-haired man with a thick walrus mustache gripped his hand and clapped him on the back. The guy looked exactly like what I imagined Sean's real dad looked like. I heard my name called and went forward. I almost stopped in my tracks as I saw my partner up at the front. He was taller than me, built like a tank. He had a crew cut and a short cropped beard. He was wearing a black tank top that showed off a very hairy chest and grey knit shorts that left little to the imagination as they hugged his crotch. His icy blue eyes crinkled at the corners when he saw me. I gulped. He stuck out his hand and I felt his big hand engulf my own.

"Good to see you again, Dylan. Been a while, hasn't it."

"Yessir, Mr. Davis," I began.

The large man laid a hand on my shoulder and spoke to the red-haired man with Sean. "Dylan here mowed my lawn for years. We are neighbors on our street." He grinned and pulled me close in a fatherly hug that seemed genuinely kind and real. He lowered his voice and spoke into my ear. "Your dad says hi, buddy. I was really glad to come and help you out. He was pleased too. We are gonna have a great day. You up for some golf?"

"Um, sure. I don't really know how to play but…"

"No worries there. Leave it to me. I'm a great teacher. Come on. Bill here is going to be in our foursome." Mr. Davis pointed to the red-haired man and Sean. "I guess you know this fellow here, right."

"Yes. Sean is in my quad."

"Excellent. Well let's go, gentlemen. Let's go hit some balls. Hey, that sounds kinda gay, don't it? Well cool. Real guys always like joking like that."

I fake laughed along with Sean who looked at me with wide amused eyes. Bill wrapped a big arm around Sean's neck and pulled him along like he was ten years old. I had a funny feeling Sean didn't mind. He leaned in close to Bill and followed him to the SUV parked out front. Soon, I was sitting in the back seat with Mr. Davis while Bill and Sean sat in front and drove to the country club. Country music blared from the speakers as Toby Keith told us all how much he loved this bar. Mr. Davis reached over and clapped a hand on my thigh.

"Your dad wanted me to make sure and tell you how much he misses you and how proud he is of you. I don't want you to get all twitter-pated with me here today. I know you are probably a bit uncomfortable with me knowing you have been sucking dicks and all that, but don't worry about it. I am not here to judge you. I'm here to play golf and just be men together. Talk about football and politics and titties." He moved his hand tenderly on my leg, dangerously close to my sack. I didn't dare move my leg. His heavy hairy knee was pressed against mine. Since both of us were wearing shorts, his scratchy leg rubbed rough against my own. Bill was deep in conversation with Sean which made me glad. I could still feel my face red from his dick sucking comment.

"How long has it been since you were working for me?"

"Um, more than year I think."

"Yeah, quite a while. I remember you all sweaty, practically getting sunstroke out there in that heat. I pulled you into the garage and got you a Coke. You had really thick armpit hair, I remember and a thick mustache. I thought you were very grown up and very masculine. You have lots of testosterone in your nuts."

I stared at the man. "Uh, thanks?"

"You know, I understand how a young man like you can get a little crossways with experimenting with friends and think that is the way it will always be. But let me tell you, once you get the real chance to eat some pussy and slide your dick in a tight cunt, you will move on from cock. It's a fine place to start learning some stuff, but you will love it."

"Okay," was all I could think to say, I was so mortified.

"Anyway, we are going to have a great day. Play some golf, get some lunch, get a couple of massages, grab a steam and a shower. You will feel like a new man."

I gulped and pushed down on my dick, smiling at Mr. Davis.

"And no more calling me Mr. Davis. It's Dick. Just call me Dick," the man said pulling me close and rubbing the back of my neck. His big hands were rough and hot. He rubbed my neck and up into my hair.

"Sure, Dick," I said leaning into him, letting my hand lightly rest on his leg.

"That's it. Just relax and enjoy hanging out with a man. Soak it in, son. It will be good for your soul. Don't worry if your pecker gets a little hard. That's just gonna happen until you learn more about pussy. Today, just enjoy being my boy."

"I will, Dick. It feels great to be your boy."

Dick mussed my hair and pulled me close and planted a wet kiss on the side of my head. "That's the ticket, sport. You know, I just had daughters. Always wanted a son. This is going to be great, just us boys hanging out and having fun."

I leaned harder against Dick's side. I could smell the faint damp musky odor from his furry pits close to my face. My leg dug in harder to his. Glancing at his lap, his cock was pressing against the fabric of his shorts, his prominent glans clearly making an appearance now. I looked at my lap and saw mine was doing the same. I spread my legs apart and rubbed my leg against Dick's. He pressed back against mine.

"I knew you just needed to hang out with a dad like me. Don't get me wrong, your father is a good man but he isn't like a real masculine guy. Your heart needs to soak up some real manly time. That's going to do so much for you to make you a real man yourself."

"That sounds good, Dad. Oh, I mean, Dick," I said leaning into him.

Dick grinned and pulled me closer. "I liked the way that sounded. You can call me Dad all you want."

I looked up front and saw Bill and Sean deep in conversation. Bill's hand was clearly rubbing Sean's leg. Through the crack in the seat, I could see the bulge in Sean's shorts and Bill's hand close by. Sean's hand was resting on the man's leg. He turned back to me and raised his eyebrows and smiled.

Fifteen minutes later, I was flying down the path on a golf cart toward the first tee. As we teed up the first shot, Dick took a long time in helping me position my hips and hands. He stood behind me and wrapped his arms around me, snuggling close as he showed me how to make my swing the best. He pressed himself close to me and I could feel the hardness of his penis against my ass as he helped me with the swing. I looked over at Sean who was staring and casually fondling the front of his shorts. After I took my shot, which was okay for a total golf virgin, Dick took his shot and then we moved out of the way for Bill and Sean. Bill took a chapter from Dick's book and stood close behind Sean and went through the movements of a correct swing. Sean's cock was so hard, it poked straight out from his crotch. Dick leaned close to my ear and whispered.

"That boy likes golf almost as much as dick, don't you think?" he snickered patting my ass again. I laughed and leaned back against him. "Damn, you are a great kid, Dylan. I'm so glad I get to be your mentor."

"Me too, Dad. I feel way manlier with you around me like this," I said. Dick patted my ass again, this time leaving his hand resting there. My penis swelled again.

By the time we were over on the far side of the course on the sixth hole, Dick had downed three beers and insisted that I have two of my own. I wasn't old enough but he said rules like that were for pussies and a boy with as much hair under his arms as I had was certainly old enough to drink a Coors Light. I eagerly drank the beer, my first experience with the stuff, and enjoyed how it went to my head and my crotch. By the time we were near the tee, I was squirming and needing to pee badly.

We pulled up at the tee along with Bill and Sean. Bill rose from the cart and bellowed, "I don't know about you boys, but my eyeballs are swimming I need to piss so bad."

"I need to piss like a Mexican racehorse," Dick said. Sean laughed. "Come on, boys. Let's go water the pine trees."

We followed the men into the woods near the hole and followed their lead. "Help me water this little fellow," Bill said pulling Sean over to the lodge pole pine in front of him. He fished out a long uncut penis and slid the skin back to reveal a huge shiny pink head. Sean pulled his dick out and stood surprisingly close and sent his stream of urine along with Bill's to the bark of the tree.

"Come on, son. Bet your balls are about to float away too," Dick said pulling out his penis and balls. The thick seven inch member lay on the huge furry balls and rose in the air, soon spurting out a clear stream of straw colored urine. I pulled out my dick and let my piss soar into the air, mixing with Dicks in little splashes. "I always wanted to have a boy to piss outdoor with. Shit, Dylan. Your cock is impressive. No wonder that boyfriend of yours wanted to suck you off all the time. Did you get that whole monster up his shithole?"

I was dumbfounded. "Uh, yeah. I mean, yeah, I cornholed him with the whole thing, balls deep."

"Fuck a duck. You know, that must open up your sinuses to feel that big boy pumping up your keister. You dump your nut in his boyhole?"

"Sure. I filled him up good," I said. I had stopped pissing but stood facing Dick with my cock in my hand, slowly sliding my fingers up and down the shaft just as he was.

"Damn, son. Looking at that big cock of yours makes me so proud. You are going to fuck girls like a motherfucker when I get done with you. I am going to teach you some tricks that will drive them crazy." Dick reached out and gently touched my cock. "Fuck, that's a goddamn horse cock, son. Your dad's dick that big?"

I shrugged my shoulders. I knew my brother had a pretty big dick but I never remembered seeing my father's penis erect or anything. Out of the corner of my eye, I saw Sean and Bill standing with hands on hips, their penises out in the wind, both hard and saluting proudly.

"Okay, okay. We gonna stay here all day stroking off together or we gonna finish this game?" Dick said pulling his cock back inside his shorts. We all followed suit and soon were teeing off on the next hole.

The bright Central Oregon sun was hot and soon we were sweating and our shirts were sticking to us as we worked our way through the next few holes. By the time we were on hole twelve, Sean and I pulled our shirts off. Soon, Bill and Dick did the same. Dick's chest was solid, dark hair ran from his neck down his torso and disappeared into his shorts. His nipples were large and brown. Soft hair covered his shoulders and there was a thick triangle of salt and pepper hair that rode right above his ass crack and disappeared into the man's shorts. Dick's ass was big and round. His calves were tanned and covered in hair. Bill was mostly smooth except for a fine dusting of red hair on his belly that got thick and darker red as it disappeared into his shorts. His legs were covered in the same thick red hair. Sean's chest was fairly tanned and freckled. He had a patch of red in the middle of his chest that spread down in a thick line into his shorts. He had a triangle of fur on his lower back as well. Seeing it above his big bubble butt made my cock swell. *What was it about this guy?* I was tanned and not too scrawny. My chest was smooth but I had a nice carpet of dark fur on my belly. My pits were thick and dark. My legs were nicely furry.

My ass was round and full, the waistband of my shorts rode up on my butt as my shorts hung low.

We finished up our round with Bill and Sean sneaking ahead of me and Dick by two strokes. That meant Dick bought the lunch, which didn't seem to bother him at all. We pulled our shirts back on and sat on the deck of the country club watching the Deschutes River pour by over chattering rocks with white foamy currents. Dick bought us all mimosas and we drank three of them before we were finished with the chicken salad croissants. My head was spinning by the time we got ready to leave. Dick put his arm around me and steadied me.

"Come on, Killer. Let's go get cleaned up and get that massage," he said guiding me to the locker room.

We found lockers in the cool locker room and began to undress. I smiled seeing Dick standing in front of me wearing an old jock that was stained and worn out. The pouch was saggy and full, trying in vain to corral his massive testicles. I looked over at Sean and smiled as I watched him bend over and slide out of his shorts and underwear. His penis was thick and heavy lying on his furry red sack. Bill undressed and I was struck how much these two were alike, other than the uncircumcised penis hanging low between Bill's furry legs. Dick must have seen me staring.

"Yeah, that elephant trunk of Bill's is pretty upsetting. Try not to stare at it, son. It'll make you go blind," Dick said with a snicker.

I looked at Dick standing at his locker, his husky muscled body hard and solid, covered in hair. His cock was more than half hard. His balls hung low, each one the size of a big plum. He smiled and took in my naked body, raising an eyebrow. "Shit, boy. That horse cock of yours looks even bigger when you are bare ass, kid. Come on, let's hit the showers.

I grabbed my towel and followed my naked mentor. The shower area was thick with steam. It appeared that most of the stalls were full. There were two at the end just coming open as naked men strode from them drying off their bodies as they disappeared into the clouds of steam.

"Sean and I can wait until you are done," I offered, staring at the showers.

"Nonsense. We'll just double up. There's tons of room. Right, Bill? In the Navy, we were packed in a lot closer than this with all the other sailors in the showers," Dick said.

"Sure were. You could wash the other guy's sack just by scratching your ass most of the time," Bill said. His penis was shamelessly erect, foreskin pulled back and dick head shining brightly. "Come on, Sean. I'll let you wash my nuts." Sean smiled and followed the man into the shower.

"You okay bathing with me, son?" Dick asked. "I know it may push some buttons for you but real men just shower together sometimes."

"It's fine, Dick. Been a while since I bathed with my dad."

"That's the spirit. I bet your dad washed your butt for you when you did."

"Sure did. My balls too," I said brazenly, keeping my voice much quieter than the men did.

I followed Dick into the large cubicle and stood under the water. He pumped the shower gel into his hands and began to rub it on my back. His thick fingers worked on the knots in my neck and moved down my back to my ass. He moved back up to my pits and soaped them up, sliding around in front and rubbing my chest and back down to my belly. His hands slid down and soaped up my pubic hair and then wrapped around my rigid penis and balls. He rolled each testicle in his fingers, talking to me about testicular self-exams and how to check your balls for lumps. He was methodical and worked on each nut for a full minute. My cock was so hard. He gripped the shaft and stroked it back and forth, commenting again on how proud my dad should be of my penis. Then he grabbed some more shower gel and his fingers slid down my crack and parted my ass. He massaged my hole and then pressed a finger inside. I sucked in my breath as a second and third finger slid in beside it.

"Real important to keep your shithole as clean as you can. Ought to be able to eat dinner off your asshole, son. No skid marks or nasty underwear. See, it feels good too to clean up down there. Okay, now your turn to do me."

The big man turned me around and I looked him in the eyes. They were smiling and crinkled at the corners. He wrapped his arms around me and pulled me close.

demanded. "Get your tongue in that hole." I obeyed and began to eat his manhole until it was dripping with my spit. "My God, you love my shitter you little cunt. If your dad had fed you his asshole like this, I bet you would have been glad to fuck a girl. Get down on your knees again," he ordered.

I looked up into his face that was fierce with rage. He gripped his penis and sent a hot blast of piss into my face and mouth. "That's it, queer boy. Drink my piss, you shit. I'll wash your faggot mouth with my dad piss."

My eyes burned as I gulped and swallowed the hot, nutty liquid. I looked up at him with sorrowful eyes, eyes that were betrayed and hurt. At the same time, my cock was bursting with hardness. I had never been this turned on. I gripped the man's firm, furry ass and swallowed gulp after gulp of his piss. As he finished, he slapped me in the face with his hard cock.

"Holy Hell, you are more of a fairy than I ever thought. You love this cock, don't you? You love me feeding it to you and making you my bitch. Your dad told me about the unnatural affection you and your friend, Ben had together. Sounds like you have been a cock-gobbler for a long time. I knew when you were sitting there in my garage; your legs all spread apart, your dick all hard as I rubbed your back. I watched you stare at my crotch. I would scratch my balls and your mouth would open like a whore. I knew then you were a fag. I should have mounted you right then and there, split your ass wide open. Well, it's never too late to teach a cocksucker a lesson. Come on, son. Time for our massage."

I scrambled to my feet and washed my face off under the water before we left. I pulled the towel around my waist. It stuck out obscenely in front of me, my dick flopping all over the place as I padded after Dick. He wore his towel low around his waist, his butt crack showing. We made our way to the massage area. I looked around and saw Bill marching Sean by the arm toward the massage rooms holding on to one arm. Sean's face was red and stricken and I knew he had just endured the same ordeal as me. His dick was similarly hard. He looked at me briefly, then glance away, embarrassed.

"Hey Sergio. How's it going? Got a two-for thing today. Me and my boy here are both wanting a good rub down. You got an amigo that can help out?"

The small brown man grinned widely and disappeared, reappearing with another Latino man with big muscles and strong hands.

"This is Lucero. He can massage your son. You want to pull the curtain for the privacy?" Sergio asked gripping the white sheet that hung above the massage table.

"No, that's not necessary, amigo. We don't have any secrets, right son?"

I nodded wondering what in the world I was agreeing to now.

"Um, just the regular massage today, senor? Si?

"Now, no need for that, Sergio. My boy here is plenty old enough to enjoy a total massage, just like you give me every time. In fact, you and your buddy Lucero need to make it extra special today. It's his first time and he is very ready, if you catch my drift."

"Si, Senor Dick. We give you both the good time massage, for sure."

"That's the ticket, Paco," Dick said in his most offensively racist voice possible it seemed to me. He pulled out a wad of twenties and laid it on the table. Sergio picked up the cash and slid it inside a drawer.

Dick tossed his towel on the chair and lay naked on the table on his belly. Sergio draped a small sheet across his butt. Dick laid his head on his hands and stared at me with a shit-eating grin. "Let's go, son," he said. "Snap to it."

I dropped my towel, holding my hand over my swollen penis and lay on the other massage table. I looked into Dick's face trying to figure out what this was all about. Lucero draped a small sheet over my ass and was soon drizzling massage oil on my back and beginning to work the kinks out. I saw Sergio disappear and then come back. He stood on the far side of Dick and was working on his back. I opened my eyes and looked over at Dick. My eyes popped open wide as I saw that Sergio was naked working diligently on Dick's back and arms, his half-hard penis bobbing as he worked on my surrogate dad. Lucero pulled my hand back and was softly kneading it in his hands. The feel was exquisite. As he put my hand down and reached for some more oil, my hand touched the bare flesh of his sack grazing my fingers. It was warm and soft and covered with black fur. I swallowed and felt my rectum contract as I realized a naked man was massaging me. Dick seemed to be practically asleep as Sergio's hands made their way down his legs to his feet and then back up to his ass. The brown hands pulled the cheeks apart and rubbed oil inside his crack and taint. I stopped breathing as I watched Sergio's face disappear into Dick's ass and feast on the big man's fleshy knot. Dick moaned loudly and spread his legs and rose up so his ass was tight against Sergio's face. In the next moment, I felt strong hands pull my cheeks apart and a warm, wet tongue penetrate my anus. I froze then melted into the amazing tongue ministry of Lucero. He pulled my ass far apart, sliding his oiled fingers deep inside. I finally realized there were four thin fingers sliding in and out of my spent hole, causing me to practically black out from the passion. Lucero moved over closer to me. I saw his penis was as hard as mine, the heavy foreskin pulled back to reveal a shining red cock, glistening with precum. I looked over at Sergio who was sliding his fingers in and out of Dick's ass with the precision of a surgeon.

"Oh yeah, amigo. That's the spot. Mmmm, fuck me, just like that Viet Cong whore's fingers on my 'prostrate'" Dick's face was lifted in ecstasy off the table as he shifted his weight back and forth, fucking himself deeper on Sergio's fingers. I could see his cock had leaked a gallon of precum on the smooth leather of the table.

"Turn over now, Mr. Dick. Time for happy ending," Sergio commanded in a soft voice. Dick spun around on his back, his cock slapping against his furry belly. It was rock hard and throbbing. Sergio poured on a dose of massage oil and began to work his penis in his fist with fluid grace while Dick squealed with delight.

Lucero grabbed my arm and pulled me around and looked at me with a kind smile. "Time for your happy ending too," he said. His oiled hands gripped my penis and began to massage and stroke my member with stunning speed and effectiveness.

I couldn't take my eyes off of Dick and Sergio. I watched the small man climb up and straddle Dick's belly, lowering his mouth down to the turgid penis that was ready to explode. He swallowed Dick's dick and to my amazement, Dick raised up and gripped Sergio's cock and slipped it in his mouth. He fastened his face to the small man's penis and sucked like a Hoover while Sergio did the same. Dick's fingers slid into Sergio's anus as he sucked. The men rocked and gulped and swallowed and moaned. I hardly noticed that Lucero had climbed up on the table and swallowed my own dick. I looked up and saw the man's thick cock hovering above my nose. I grabbed for it and swallowed him balls deep. He skillfully began to fuck my mouth as he sucked my cock and massaged my balls. From the corner of my eye, I saw Dick slam his crotch up into Sergio's face and groan like a bull in heat. Dick held Sergio's penis and I saw a blast of semen shoot from the tip of his cock and into Dick's open mouth. That was it. I orgasmed in a volcano of sperm that blasted out of me into Lucero's talented mouth. I was aware of hot, salty semen filling my own mouth and I hungrily lapped it up and sucked and nursed on Lucero's cock until he eased out of my mouth and stood beside me, leaning down to plant a cum-flavored kiss on my lips. I looked over at Dick who was lying on his side, propped up on his hand, his spent penis slowly leaking semen on the table.

"See son, that's what a real man enjoys. I know sometimes there are female masseuses to go to, but these guys know what they are doing and they know how to keep quiet about it. If you have the urge to get your nut off with a boy, then this is how you do it. Go to a professional and pay for it and no one is the wiser. So a cock-gobbler like you can get his jollies but not be out there sucking every Tom's Dick and Harry. You know what I mean?"

I was so overwhelmed and overloaded, I just nodded. Dick swung his legs over the table and walked over to me and wrapped me in his arms as I sat up. His face was tight against mine. "Sorry if that shit in the shower got a little intense. Just part of what we are asked to do to try and get you boys to change your thinking, go for the puss instead of the pecker." He held me tight and rubbed my back and head, with genuine affection and tenderness. "I really love you being my son, Son," he said. "Let's go get that steam." He reached out and took my hand and led me like a little boy to the steam room. "Hey Sergio, we got this for the next twenty minutes, right?" Dick asked.

"Yessir, Mr. Dick," Sergio said with a smile struggling back into this white t-shirt.

Lucero was still standing around in shock, holding his underwear and the wad of cash that Dick somehow had handed out. I looked around and saw Sean and Bill following us toward the steam room. Sean had a look on his face that was unmistakably one of 'I've just shot my load' contentment. He was holding the towel around his waist. Bill didn't even bother, he just barreled naked toward the steam room with a confident look of anticipation on his face. We walked into the steam room. Another group of four men were in the room. As my eyes adjusted to the steam, I was shocked to see Manny and JaMarcus with their mentors sitting naked on towels in the moist, liquid heat. One look at Manny's face told me everything I was wondering. That same shamed look mixed with the sensory overload of sex, and lots of it.

"Gentlemen," the large black man with Manny spoke. "Glad you could join us. Had a fun day, fellows?" he asked nodding toward me. My mouth was too dry to speak but I nodded and grinned like an idiot. "Your little friend here had quite a day himself, that right Manny?"

"Yessir," Manny mumbled not making eye contact with any of us. I wondered if they had had the same experiences that Sean and I had. JaMarcus was quiet as well. The small Asian man sat beside him and his hand rested in JaMarcus's lap against the man's cock that was swollen and erect.

"JaMarcus has some amazing skills. I think the rest of these boys must be the same," he said.

"You got that right, Tanaka," Bill said pulling Sean's head over and planting a big kiss on the top of his head. "This Irish sword swallower can't get enough dick, that's for sure." I could see Sean's face redden even in the dim, steamy air.

"Same for my Eye-Talian Stallion, here. He gobbles down cock like he's at an all you can eat buffet," Dick said. "These boys are gonna get their fill of nut and finally decide it's time to move on to pussy."

Alarm bells rang in my head.

"Okay, faggots. Here's how this works. You are gonna start servicing us. Every time the timer on my phone dings, you move on to the cock on your right."

I stared at my friends. Manny shook his head. "I don't want to…"

The black man slapped him on the back of his head. "Shut the fuck up, you sorry sack of shit and get my cock back in yo' mouth." Manny sunk to the floor and took the huge penis into his mouth and began to suck. I fell to the floor and moved in-between Dick's legs and found his cock was hard again. I sucked him all the way to his balls and bobbed my head up and down as he forced his penis deep into my mouth. I could hear Sean slurping on Bill beside me. Somewhere down the line,

JaMarcus was blowing Mr. Tanaka. Sweat poured from my face and ran down my butt crack as I bent over blowing Dick. A small chirping sound filled the tiled room.

"Okay, swap ladies. Move down the line."

I moved to my right and stared at the large uncut cock in Bill's lap coated with Sean's spit. "Let's go, Junior," he said slapping my lips with the thick meat. I opened my mouth wide and swallowed his cock and began to suck. As I licked and sucked, Bill pulled my head down hard, gagging me on his cock. He fucked in and out of my mouth and finally grunted and sent a load of semen into my mouth: hot, sour, and thick.

"Christ on a crutch, this boy can suck," Bill said. The alarm dinged.

I moved to my right and looked up at Mr. Tanaka. He grabbed my face and pushed it down on his cock. It was smaller than the others I had been sucking, but he made up for it with violent thrusts that still went to the back of my throat. I heard more gagging and retching. I heard other men climaxing and sending a blast of sperm into the mouth of the guy blowing them. *How can these guys cum so much*, I thought? My mouth filled with Tanaka nut as the alarm dinged. I staggered to my feet and felt my arm pulled toward the other side of the room.

"Assume the position, pansy boy," the big black man rumbled. I stared at his penis, easily more than eight inches. I opened my mouth and felt the man's cock hit the back of my throat in no time. He gripped my head and began to fuck my face with a fast rhythm. Snot and spit flowed from my mouth as he thrust again and again. When his semen erupted, it shot out my nose like a fountain. The alarm dinged again. We looked around wondering if we were supposed to move around the circle again.

"Okay, fags. You like sucking dick so much, let's see you work on each other's cock." Bill said.

I found myself face to face with Manny and he sunk to his knees and took my cock into his mouth. I put my hands on his head and slowly fucked his mouth. His tongue and mouth were amazingly talented. His hands pulled my ass apart. I felt strong hands pull them apart even further. I looked around and saw Tanaka move to eat my ass, sliding his tongue deep within my anus.

"Oh God," I moaned.

The man ate deep and hungrily until my climax was nearing the tipping point. The big black man moved over close and pulled Manny off my cock and pushed Sean forward to feed him his rock hard erection. The black man gripped Manny's ass and opened it wide, exposing his hole.

"Eat that Mexican cunt," he ordered me. I moved down and slid my mouth and tongue onto Manny's soggy anus and began to lap and munch on his hole. It was thick with black fur and very open. My tongue easily slid inside and fucked his manhole. Soon I was being roughly pulled up again.

"Fuck his cunt, now faggot!" the man screamed. I lined up my penis with Manny's hole and pressed in hard. His muscle popped open and he groaned as I slid inside. It was tight and hot. The idea of fucking this dad and married man was fucking intense. Sweat was practically blinding me as I fucked deep and hard. I felt someone behind me now eating my own ass as I pumped in and out of Manny. Within a minute, I felt a hard penis rub on my hole and press inside. It hurt like hell, stretching me wide apart and burning my gut. I saw JaMarcus's dark hands wrap around me as he fucked deep within my stretched hole causing me to fuck even deeper into Manny's ass. The small man groaned even louder. I saw the big black man pull Sean over and bend him over and slam his monster cock into Sean's soggy hole. Sean screamed and held on to the tile bench as the man rode his ass like a bull. I watched Dick disappear behind the black man and soon he was fucking his ass in rhythm with the man fucking Sean.

"Goddamn I love your black manhole," Dick bellowed thrusting in and out in a hard constant pounding.

Bill moved around and slid his cock into Manny's mouth again and fucked it hard while I continued to ride his ass. "Mmmmff," was all I could hear from him. Soon, I felt my balls draw up to my belly and my semen exploded into Manny's ruined hole, leaking in a pool of white pancake mix onto the floor of the steam room. JaMarcus gripped me tight and I felt his cock swell in my stretched hole and blast his jizz deep within me. Bill's climax filled Manny's mouth with another huge load of nut that leaked from the sides of his mouth. Sean cried out as the big black man slammed hard against him, depositing his seed within the red-haired boy's stretched pussy. We fell against each other in a heap of heaving sweaty flesh.

In a few moments, our mentors were pulling us to our feet and marching us back to the showers. Dick pulled me into a stall and turned on the water. He gently washed the semen from my face and soaped my penis and ass, cleaning the sperm from my body. He held me tightly, rubbing my body and washing me as a dad might do with a small boy. Two, then three fingers easily slid inside my asshole. He turned me around and I held on to the wall as he entered me. His cock felt good and solid in my hole. His belly and balls made ringing slapping sounds as he bred me one last time, sending another load of semen into my ravaged hole. As he finished fucking me, he pulled me around and kissed me on the mouth.

"See, Son. That's what your life as a cocksucker is going to be like. You know it's not that good for you. You will want to try pussy and not be a cum swallowing bitch. Right?"

I nodded, more in weary resignation than agreement. I was exhausted and my belly was full of semen and piss. And I had never been happier in my life.

The mentors dropped us off at the center in the early evening. The four of us moved robotically into the cafeteria and sat in front of our plates of food, ravenous and mortified. No one spoke. From the looks of things around the room, most of the young men must have had the same kind of day. Everywhere you looked, hang-dog faces, shame, and no eye contact ruled the place. I noticed most of the guys had flushed, worn-out faces. I wondered how many of them had spent their day sucking dicks like we had and so much more. We all put our dinner trays away and made our way back to the quad. All the guys disappeared into our bedroom. I lay in my bed trying to make sense of the day, feeling drained and weak. I slid my hand inside my underwear and touched my penis. It was hard again. *My God,* I thought, *How can I still be horny?* My door opened and I saw Sean standing in the shaft of light, his body practically glowed. The twin mounds of his ass were tightly framed and hugged by the Calvin Klein briefs he wore. I sat up in bed and smiled weakly and motioned for him to come in. He walked to the bed and slid in beside me, spooning me close and wrapping his arms around me. I felt his erection press against my ass. It felt good.

"What the fuck..." was all he said.

I wrapped my hand back around his ass and pulled him closer. His face rested on mine. I could feel the warm breath flowing over me as he breathed. His hand slid down and found my cock and gently teased it through my shorts. He wiggled his fingers under the elastic and found my penis and rubbed the leaking tip over the head and tiny lips of my dick. His lips lightly kissed the side of my face. For some reason it was hotter than all the big mouth kissing from the dads today.

"Do you feel like fucking a girl in the pussy?" I whispered as he fondled me.

"Fuck no. Do you?"

"Not after today. If there was any doubt I love dick, those fuckers made sure I was a cocksucker for sure. All I can think about is how much I want you to fuck me right now."

"I know. Before today, I was wondering if maybe I could start to just focus on vagina and live like a straight guy. Do you think they actually believe all that shit could turn us off dick instead of making us crave it more?"

I gripped my underwear and slid them off my ass and pressed back against Sean. He pulled his dick out and let it rest in my crack, sliding back and forth near my hole. He pushed my shorts the rest of the way down then pulled his own off as well. I turned my head toward him and his soft lips and scratchy face slid against mine. Our kiss was deep and passionate. I gripped my right knee and pulled my leg up and apart. Sean spat into his hand and rubbed it on his dick and against my sore hole. I gasped as his large penis penetrated me, sliding forward until his balls banged against my ass. He held still for a moment and then began to thrust gently inside me. It felt good, it felt...right to be riding his cock.

"Goddamn, I am falling for you, brother," I whispered. "We're gonna end up in that fucking chair, aren't we?"

Sean was breathing hard. "Oh yeah," he said as he unloaded his balls into my ass.

Chapter 6
The Vagina Dialogues

I woke in the early morning hours before it was light. I turned and smiled to find Sean still there. I slid under the covers and took his penis into my mouth. He stirred awake and soon returned the favor. We devoured one another, sending a warm protein breakfast down each other's gullet before settling back into a tight embrace with kisses and caresses.

"You know," he said, "You probably won't believe this, but this thing we are doing here. It's more to me than just getting some dick. I'm kind of crazy about you, I think."

I pulled him close. "Thank goodness. I thought it was just me. From the minute I walked into this place and saw you smiling at me, I've been lost. You are making me fall for you as well. "

Sean's hands rubbed up and down my back and gripped my butt. I looked deep into those blue-green eyes of his and grinned. I was pretty sure this wasn't what the founding fathers of this fucked up place had in mind. I was definitely falling in love, I thought. But there wasn't a vagina in sight. I kissed Sean again, feeling my cock rise as I did. The kisses were deep and warm, our lips and tongues fit together in an entrancing dance. I held his face and moved around from his brow to his eyes to his nose and back to his lips. They were thick and full, his face was meaty and manly. His eyes sparkled in the early morning light as he grinned at me. He gripped my penis and squeezed it tightly in his hand.

"I kind of want to ride this big boy," he said scrambling up onto my lap. He spit into his hand and rubbed the saliva on my cock and I felt it wedged into the warm recess of his ass crack. Sean's eyes closed and he wiggled his big butt around and I sighed as my dick disappeared inside his tight rosebud.

"Holy shit, that's a big dick," he whispered as he sat firmly on my balls, impaling my cock fully inside his rectum. I gripped his waist and began to pump in and out of the tight grip of his ass. Sean pumped his cock as he rode my dick, his face in deep delight. I could tell he was hitting a sweet spot up inside, his mouth gaped open and he stopped pumping his dick, just riding my cock instead, rocking back and forth. His mouth opened wider and he grunted and a thick blast of spunk shot across my belly, his hands high in the air. I gasped and unloaded my nuts into his clinching butt that milked blast after blast out of my penis.

"Fuck, y'all going after it pretty damn early today," JaMarcus said climbing on the bed and wrapping his arms around Sean. I looked to the side and saw Manny's hairy legs kneel beside my head. He was naked and his penis was hard with morning wood. He straddled my head and slid his dick into my mouth as he bent forward to kiss Sean. He pulled away and licked up the sperm on my belly and then pumped his cock in and out of my mouth as he made out with Sean. My dick slid from Sean's cummy hole and I heard him groan as JaMarcus slid inside.

"Oh fuck, you are sawing me in half with that thing," Sean complained as JaMarcus penetrated him to his balls."

"Oh please, bitch. I know your ass can take a lot more than this. I seen you fucked like a whore yesterday by Sgt. Hall."

Manny laughed and drove his dick deeper into my mouth, grunting as his early morning load flowed down my throat. "Dios Mio, hermano," he said. "You have a fucking talented mouth, my friend."

Manny's semen was warm and spicy but tasted good and manly and made me instantly want more. We scrambled from underneath Sean and JaMarcus and I pulled his ass apart and sucked on his asshole to his delight. He groaned and leaned his head down on the bed as I ate his ass. The river of spit from my mouth made the thick black hairs in his ass crack matted and wet. I climbed up and aimed my penis at his brown pucker and leaned forward until the muscle relaxed and I slid in. I joined JaMarcus's fuck rhythm, pounding on Manny's tight pucker like a jackhammer. The man reached around and pulled my ass toward him, trying to get more and more of cock inside him. When I released my jizz, I pulled out and coated his crack with thick white paste. I mopped it up with the head of my penis and then shoved it back inside his hole, breeding him deep and hard.

"Holy fuck, Dylan. You know how to fuck a man," Manny said turning back to me with a grin. I leaned down and kissed him, his lips hot and full. He pulled me down and wrapped me in a bear hug and continued to kiss me, his tongue filling my mouth as he did. In a few moments, the four of us lay heaving in a heap on the bed.

"You think they have cameras in the quads?" Sean said as his head lay between JaMarcus's thighs, a clear mustache of semen on his upper lip.

"I been wondering about that myself," he said in a deep early morning voice.

"I don't think so," Manny said. "I think they would have already crashed down the door with all this shit we've been doing. Fuck, I am loving dick more now than I ever did before I came to this crazy place.

"Me too. It's all I want now," I said leaning up and licking the tip of Manny's penis that still dripped with his sperm.

"Shit, I just wonder what's in store for us today," Sean said. "I don't know if I can take another fuck-a-thon like yesterday. My ass is wrecked."

"Poor baby. Don't worry, I'll kiss it and make it better," Manny said with a laugh.

The four men cleaned up and headed to the dining hall for breakfast. They were greeted toothily by Saul who seemed almost incoherent with happiness this morning. "Greetings, gentlemen. Today is a great day. I know you will be very excited with the announcements." I honestly thought he was going to stroke out with so much energy exuding from his face. "Hey, Dylan, can I have a word?"

"Sure."

"Just come back to my office after breakfast before the announcements."

I finished my French toast and bacon and coffee and headed back to Saul's office. I almost ducked into the bathroom again as I saw Doug headed in there. The man smiled and gave his crotch a slight rub as he pushed the door open. But I was fairly well satiated this morning with cock and just headed on to the office, much to Doug's dismay.

I pushed the door open and Saul motioned me in, clearly listening to a voice mail on his phone. I came in and stood in front of his desk. He hung up and he moved around to the front of his desk as well. He sat on the edge of it in front of me.

"So how did it go yesterday, brother?"

I was taken aback. "Um, it was good. A bit unexpected and all that."

Saul put his hands up on my shoulders. "I remember my mentor day. My cornhole had never felt like that before," he said with candid honesty. "How many times did you get fucked?"

"I…honestly I can't remember. Plenty. Dick is a pretty passionate guy."

"Yes, he's one of our best mentors. He always participates. He certainly unloaded his balls into me quite a few times."

"Really?"

"Oh yeah. He made me swallow so much semen, I finally got tired of the stuff."

I smiled and nodded. "Don't know that I'm quite there yet."

"Oh you will be soon enough."

"You don't say. Um, is there anything else?"

Saul's smile faded slightly. "I know it's not easy, but you and Sean and your other quad mates need to lay off the fucking. You aren't here to be faggots together night and day. You are supposed to be helping one another be real men." Saul's hand shot out and gripped my cock and balls like a vice. "If you keep being cocksuckers, you are gonna get the chair and I don't want to see you there." His hand released my dick then slid down the front of my shorts and inside my underwear and grabbed my junk again. "You've got to get your shit together and stop acting like a queer all the time. Your dick shouldn't be all hard right now and leaking precum. You have to think like a real straight man."

I pushed on his hand. "Then maybe you need to stop fondling my cock and I will act more straight. What is it with you? Why don't we just fuck and get it over with. I know you want to."

Saul's hand pulled out of my shorts and slapped me across the face with a blinding blow. I staggered back holding my face, staring at him.

"I'm sorry to have to do that, Dylan. But you have to snap out of it. It's time to take all this more seriously or you will be in the chair before you know it."

"Fuck you and the chair. Go ahead and put me in it. I'm fine with that."

A chime sounded indicating it was time to begin the announcements. I turned to leave. "If you ever lay a hand on me like that again, I will fucking sue you and this goddamn house or horrors." I left without looking back. My face was red with fury as well as the slap when I got back to the table. Sean stared and started to ask, but I just shook my head and mouthed 'Later' to him. My mind was spinning. *How the fuck did Saul know about us boning one another all the time unless...*

The center director was at the microphone and began with the morning announcements. Most were routine reminders and general housekeeping sorts of things. "And finally, gentlemen. This evening, we will be hosting our first ladies night in our pub. This is a great time for you to hone your skills of seduction and conquest. One of these ladies could be your ticket to heterosexual bliss. So we expect all of you to be there and be prepared."

Several of the other workers at the center began to circulate through the lunch room and deposited fist-fulls of bright colored condoms on the tables. The young men at the tables looked embarrassed and sheepishly grabbed a few of the prophylactics and shoved them into their pockets. Manny grabbed some of the rubbers and leaned over to me.

"Oh man, we could have used some of these this morning," he said.

The four of us made it back to the quad and I wasted no time in telling them all what Saul had said. Sean and Manny looked stricken. JaMarcus was defiant.

"I told y'all they was spying on us. Fuck me."

I spoke up. "You know all of us think this place is bullshit. None of us believe it can work and more than that, we have nothing that needs to be changed. We are what we are, and that's it. I don't care if they put me in the fucking chair. I'm not sure how, but I can't believe all the big wigs at this shit place know about us fucking around and are just letting it happen. Maybe Saul is just a pervy stalker and is peeking in our goddamn windows. I am going to continue to sleep with Sean. I like it and it feels good." I walked over to Sean and held out my hand. He looked up at me with a look of fear and worry. But in the end, he gripped my hand and smiled.

"I'm with you, brother," he said. I smiled and felt my heart grow light.

Later that evening, after a full day of sports with sweaty men, lectures on being a real man, agonizingly horrific how-to videos on successfully dating the woman of your dreams, we loaded up in vans and were transported to Sunriver Resort. My not-quite-straight brothers and I were looking our best, like a one-sided prom night. Tonight, we would endure a session of speed dating and possibly even find a girl who was so enamored with us in a few moments, she would be willing to sleep with us. For a program that was supposedly so entrenched in religion, I found this idea of Walmart Black Friday shopping for a date totally Neanderthal. Shouldn't this take a nice long time? Don't people need to fall in love? I mean, okay, for guys sometimes it's fun to just get our rocks off and I guess girls feel the same, even though they don't have rocks. It seemed the folks at Straight Ahead were mostly interested in teaching guys to put a notch in their belt to signal to the world…"Look at me! I put my pee-pee in a vajay-jay."

Sean sat beside me in the van. His big leg was pressed against mine. Our hands were actually touching as we drove, which made my dick half hard. I looked at him and he was sweating around his lips and forehead.

"You okay, big guy?" I whispered.

"Yeah. I just don't want to do this. You know what I mean?"

"Oh yeah. It's the stupidest thing we've done and that is including going golfing for dong with the dads. It's humiliating, like a slave auction or a Sadie Hawkins dance or something," I agreed.

"If you hit it off with a girl tonight, are you going to sleep with her?"

"I can't imagine that happening. But I don't mind having some fun with a nice girl. I love hanging with girls."

"Me too, sort of. What if she wants to blow you or something?"

I shrugged my shoulders. "Not sure I would get hard, but it might be fun. If she's cute or at least fun to be with."

"Man, you are way cooler than me. I just feel like dying already."

I gripped Sean's hand. "You are cool. You are a fucking smokin' hot man who is going to make some girl all wet down there. Just pretend you are in a play or musical. You like acting. Just do the role and see if you can enjoy it along the way. You and me, we both know it's bullshit but it will get us out of here if we act like we are trying."

"I'm tired of living a lie," Sean said, tears filling his blue-green eyes. "I'd rather just learn how to be a good husband for you."

My face flushed red. I had never heard him talk like this. "Me too, buddy. I'm falling in love with you too. I can't even pretend not to. But try to do the straight thing tonight. Just be charming and have fun. If you end up alone or whatever with a girl, just do what the straight guys do and see if they want to fuck. If they do, then rise to the occasion. Then come back home to me and I will make you forget all about them," I whispered moving my hand to his crotch. I noticed the boy across from me watching. He smiled and gave me a small thumbs-up when I looked at him. I smiled back.

We disembarked at the resort and filed into one of the large banquet rooms. It was set up with dozens and dozens of tables. Two chairs were facing each other with a candle in the middle of the table in between them. The guys were given numbers and told to stand over against the wall. Girls began to file in and soon they were directed to sit down. An announcement was made and the girls turned over a card in front of them. Each card was a number. The announcer told the guys to find the lady who corresponded with their number and take a seat, but to not talk. We began to mill around. I had number 22. I found the girl with that number and sat in front of her, trying not to give much eye contact. The energy in the room was erratic and oscillated between anxiety and despair. The announcer told us to look at the back of the card we had been given and work our way through the questions. We would have four minutes to visit with each girl before a bell sounded and we had to shift one seat to our right.

"Okay, ladies and gentlemen. Begin." The announcer tapped a bell with a small mallet and we all drew in a collective breath.

I looked at the girl in front of me and almost shit. My friend, Tara, smiled back. She wore a turquoise slinky top that was low cut and framed her small breasts and made them more impressive than I had seen before. Her hair was up and she wore makeup that made her look much older.

"Hi Dylan," she whispered. "I don't think that's on the card. I'm not sure we are supposed to know each other," she giggled. "How is it going here? Do you think you have started to like girls?"

I was so flummoxed, I just smiled and blurted out, "Still a sausage fest for me, Tara. But who knows, maybe you can change all that?" She giggled. "What in the hell are you doing here?"

She shrugged her shoulders. "I just wanted to meet some new guys. No one ever gives me the time of day back home."

I leaned closer. "I always did."

She blushed. "I know. I just kind of want a boy who wants to be with a girl."

I smiled and shook my head, reaching across the table to grip her hand. I noticed the girl beside her turned and her eyes opened wide taking in the sight. "You have come to the worst place in the world for that, I'm afraid."

She laughed. "You know me, I'm big on lost causes. Who knows? Maybe some poor sap here is tired of all the sausage." I laughed loud causing the speed daters on either side to stop their conversation and look at me.

"Well, if you don't find a willing victim, you can count on me," I said.

"Thanks, Dylan. You are so sweet." The bell rang and I shifted to my right still looking at Tara who smiled with twinkling eyes in my direction. I looked in front of me and a stunned blonde girl with nice big breasts and large teeth smiled at me.

"Hi," she said. "I'm Jessica."

"Hi. Dylan," I said reaching over to shake her hand. I looked down at the questions that I hadn't bothered with at all with Tara and read the first one: "Um, if you could be any animal in the wild, what would you be?" *What the fuck?*

Jessica laughed but proceeded on like she was on the Miss America pageant. "Well, I think I would want to be an Eagle. I love being free and exploring new things. I like being high too."

"Don't we all," I agreed with a smile. Jessica didn't catch the joke. So I just took my turn. "Okay, well I think I would pick a bear."

"Really. Why is that?"

"Big and furry, strong, no one fucks with them. Oh, and you get to sleep for about three months."

Jessica laughed again having no idea what in the world any of this meant, just like the rest of us. "Okay. Well, if you could have any job…"

The banal questions continued. I learned Jessica loved pink, wanted to be a makeup artist in Hollywood, and was a virgin. After that, my brain just went somewhere else. I was fine talking with her about makeup, but she meant like lipstick and eye shadow and I mean foam and latex. The next girl was a brunette and a total skeleton. I wondered if the girl had eaten a whole meal in years. Thin girls are fine but this was distracting. I kept staring at her collarbone that protruded like armor from her pearly white skin. She mentioned something about being adventurous and thinking rough sex sounded like fun. I thought it sounded like a quick trip to the hospital.

The queue of girls seemed endless. It seemed like every one of them had some hint of hope when they first began talking with you but soon that look dissolved into hopelessness or downright annoyance. I kept wondering who in the world sold these girls on the idea of speed dating with a bunch of bone smokers? I thought, that is the kind of salesman I would hire if I had a company. Forget ice to the Eskimos. The sad part of all this to me was that I thought several of the girls were really hot, fun to chat with, and would make a really amazing friend to go shopping with or out to dinner. I could tell we were all being scrutinized like crazy and I had a distinct feeling if I didn't make some sort of connection here, I was going to be sitting in the chair really soon. That thought filled me anxiety and perverse excitement too.

"Hi. Isn't this the stupidest thing ever?"

I looked up and saw another pretty blonde. She smiled and had a kind face that put you at ease immediately. I could swear I already knew her even though I didn't. I smiled back.

"Talk about hopeless causes, huh?" I said. She giggled and leaned close.

"I love my gay boyfriends back home. I have way more fun with them than the regular boys who just want me to give them a blow job and bend over at the end of a date."

"Yikes," I said. "Well it's pretty much the same with us gays except for the part where we mind giving the blow jobs and bending over." More laughter.

"You found a girl to date here tonight?"

I shrugged. "I doubt it."

She looked around the room. "I saw you standing with that cute redhead guy over there when you first came in. Any chance you boys are...?" I grimaced nervously and looked around. She reached over and gripped my hand. "No worries. He looks like the kind of guy you should be with. He fun in bed?"

I looked around hoping no one was listening. It looked like the people on either side of us were still pretending to try and do the speed dating. I cleared my throat and squeezed her hand a bit. "Yeah. Very fun."

"By the way, I'm Allison," she said looking down at her name tag and rolling her eyes. I nodded and held up the tag that hung on the lanyard around my neck. "Hi Dylan. Guess I'm not sticking to the script here."

"Thank God."

She looked around the hall and then back to me and leaned closer. "Look, this is a waste of time for all you guys...and us for that matter. But would you like to just hang out afterwards. Doesn't need to be a date. I think it would be fun to talk and pick your brain on a couple of things. That's my girlfriend over there. Not like my lesbian girlfriend, just...you know."

"Copy. I think I got it," I said with a smile rubbing my thumb on her hand. This girl was definitely fun to hang with, I thought. Other than the not having a dick thing, I could see us becoming friends for sure.

"Maybe you and your buddy with the great hair would come out with us. We are staying overnight. We could eat or go dancing or see a movie or just talk."

"That sounds pretty great, especially after this fiasco. Um, they are kind of strict that we are only supposed to hang out with girls if it is romantically leading to fornication or something like that."

Allison laughed loudly, throwing her head back in joy. Her blonde curls flowed around her shoulder and for some reason I wanted to touch her hair. That's weird, I thought. "Well I'm not sure about that, but to be honest, I could probably enjoy a little light fornicating tonight."

I couldn't help smiling. "For some reason when you talk about it, it doesn't sound half bad."

The damn bell rang. We both looked lost for a moment. "I'll find you when this mess is over," I said gripping her hand one last time. She smiled as I pulled away and moved to the next girl who looked completely hopeless. I went through the exercise with the next girl robotically but kept looking over at Allison.

"You could at least pretend to pay attention to me," the new girl snapped looking daggers at me.

"I'm not that good of a pretender," I snapped back.

"Asshole," she hissed back under her breath.

"That's the most honest thing I've heard from anyone tonight, sweetheart," I said with a grin. She folded her arms and sat in silence until the bell rang again.

The endless litany of questions and faking finally came to an end. Everyone was relieved. The announcement was made that we would take a break and then the couples were encouraged to come back and enjoy the music and dancing and see what else the night would bring. It was like some Cinderella story with much more magic desperately needed. I bolted from the table and headed out to the deck that looked out on the river. On cue, the boys and girls parted and soon the homogeneous groups were deep in talk, just not with one another. I found Sean and Manny and gave them worn-out smiles as I came close.

"That was as much fun as taking the SATs or something," Sean said.

"Or a colonoscopy," Manny said. "So stupid. I am a married guy for chrissake."

"I don't think this was well thought out at all. Not fair to these poor girls or us," I offered.

I wanted to move close to Sean and feel him wrap his arms around me. I stood close enough for my arm and shoulder to touch his. His hand was behind his back close to the railing of the deck. I moved where I was blocking the view and slid my hand into his. He gripped it.

"I want to fuck you so much right now," he said out the corner of his mouth. "I want to bend you over this bannister."

"That would probably raise an eyebrow or two. But it sounds like heaven to me. So did you find a girl to sleep with tonight?" I teased.

"Fuck no. Some were nice, some were hot. A couple were actually fun to talk to. But no, I'll save my fucking for you. What about you?"

"You know, I think I did find a girl tonight. We are going out here in a bit."

Sean's face fell and his mouth gaped open. I smiled and rubbed my fingers against his behind his back. "Relax buddy. She's just a cool girl. She has a friend too. What do you say to us going out with them, just to make it look good? I think we will have some fun."

"Who is this other girl?" Sean said suspiciously squeezing my hand. I pointed over at Allison and her friend. "I remember both of them I think," he said. "They were okay. Fine, as long as we go together. Is that even allowed?"

"It is. I asked Saul earlier today. I said it might be a good way to break the ice."

"Okay. I'm in," Sean leaned closer. "And later tonight, I will be all in, inside your sweet ass again, that is."

We walked over to the girls and I introduced Sean to Allison.

"This is Emily," Allison said nodding to her friend. Emily was short with spiky dark hair, perky round breasts, and full ruby lips. I noticed that Sean was staring at her tits that were gripped by the tight halter top dress she wore.

"Hey, Buddy. Up here. I'm up here," she said motioning for him to look at her face instead of her boobs. Sean's face went scarlet. "You sure he likes cock?" she said boldly to Allison. The girls giggled and fell against one another.

"You want to blow this joint and go have some fun?" Allison said to both of us.

We both shrugged and nodded yes. Allison stretched her hand out to me and took mine and led me out of the hall. Emily did the same with Sean. We looked like two dopey little boys going to lunch with big sister or something. I noticed that our actions certainly caught the eye of many in the crowd. Saul's face broke into a wide grin complete with a thumbs-up. Manny just stared. JaMarcus shook his head and mouthed "Hell no," to us as we left with the girls, being the first of the group to do so. I just grinned and went along with it. I loved hanging with girls so hopefully this would be fun.

We walked like couples along the sidewalks toward some of the other condos in the resort. I wondered where they were taking us. Maybe we would get in a car and head into Bend or something. There's a good gay bar then maybe we could go there, I thought. Allison moved close and wrapped her hand around my waist. I did the same holding her close thinking it felt pretty nice. There was no pressure or expectation. I looked behind me and Sean had his big arm around Emily's shoulder. He looked like a natural.

"So where we going, sweetheart?" I asked.

"Back to our room," Allison said with a lilting music in her voice.

"What?"

"Sure. That's what all this was about, wasn't it?" She moved closer under my arm.

"I kind of thought we were kidding," I said, sadness edging through my voice.

"Don't overthink this, Sport. Trust me, okay?"

"Okay. You're the boss."

"Now you're talking," Allison said with a giggle.

We made our way along the path under a dark carpet of glittering stars. I could hear Sean and Emily chatting away behind us. For all his bluster and reticence, he seemed to be doing just fine. Allison guided me up a set of stairs and down a dim corridor until we came to Room 267.

"Is there a party here or something?" Sean said cluelessly.

"Not yet, big guy. But soon," Emily said pushing him in the door with me shaking my head.

The girls' room was big looking out on the river and mountains beyond. The fireplace was going. A cozy sectional couch filled the room. There was a master suite bedroom to the left. A large Jacuzzi tub filled the space near the sliding glass doors and the fireplace. Allison disappeared and came back with a bottle of tequila. She moved around the bar, loading up a blender with juice, booze, and ice and soon frozen mango margaritas were being poured.

"Nice," Sean said. "I needed a drink bad." He gulped down a big drink and grabbed his forehead. "Fuck, ice cream headache." We all laughed as Sean rolled over on the couch and held his head. I couldn't help but notice the bulge in his pants. I saw Emily saw the same. She sat down beside him and brazenly slid her hand over and gripped his junk. Sean froze momentarily, holding his head and then he peeked out from his hands with a sly grin and opened up his big legs even wider.

"What did you find down there, sweetheart. You looking for some sausage?"

"Shut the fuck up and take off these goddamn pants," Emily said pulling off her top. Her bare breasts jiggled, pink nipples stood out in the cool air. Sean's big hands reached up and softly caressed them.

"Nice," was all he said as Emily pulled his pants open. He raised his big ass off the couch and let her slide the slacks to the floor. She gripped the pouch of his grey Calvin Klein boxer briefs and lowered her face to the cotton and breathed in deeply. *Fuck*, I thought. *This girl loves dick almost as much as I do.* My jealousy alarm was going off big time. I felt Allison's hands slide down to my lap.

"Looks like they have the idea. You want to give it a try?" As her hands touched me, I flinched. But looking at Sean's bulge, I found I was getting hard. Allison looked at my face and saw where I was staring. "It's fine to watch his cock. Shit, Emily and I are hoping you boys will fuck so we can watch…and maybe join in if you enjoy it."

I stared at her. "Really? You want to watch us fuck?"

Allison pulled her top off over her head. Her hair was wild and free. Her tits were large and round with dark areolas and nice nipples. "That's exactly what we want. Watching boys make out and suck and fuck each other is the hottest thing in the world to me, especially if I can be in the big middle of it." Her hands pulled open my pants and gripped my penis and squeezed it firmly. "Fuck, I knew you would be big, but damn."

My mind was basically short-circuiting. But as I looked over and saw Sean now naked and his hand on the back of Emily's head, force-feeding his cock to her, her brown lightly furry pussy winking from between her legs, I gave in to the moment. I pulled my shirt over my head and pushed down my pants and briefs, feeling my erection slap my belly. Allison sunk to her knees and took my penis into her mouth and began to suck. I only had eyes for Sean, though. He looked straight into my eyes with a wild expression that looked half trapped, half in heaven, still skull fucking Emily. I watched his big balls slam up and down into her chin, rivulets of spit flowing down the huge orbs that I wanted in my mouth so bad. I laid my head back, continuing to feed Allison my cock as I watched Sean do the same, his eyes like lasers into mine. Finally, he pushed up from the couch, dislodging Emily from his cock and wrapped me in his arms and began to kiss. I gripped his muscled shoulders and pulled him close. His thick lips fit into my mouth perfectly and then his tongue as well. And all the time, Emily and Allison continued to suck our cocks. We held each other tight, our hands moving down our bodies and gripping each other's chest and back as we rubbed against each other. Finally, Sean pushed me down and pushed Allison off my cock and he swallowed it. I maneuvered around and pulled Sean from Emily's grasp and swallowed his penis as well, his thick, hairy legs surrounding my face. I gripped his ass and pulled him as far into my mouth as I could take. In the middle of all this, I felt a warm mouth envelop my balls at the same time I was getting sucked off by Sean. *Damn, these girls really are into this,* I thought.

I heard Sean grunt as he continued to swallow my cock and soon, I joined him. The girls had begun to slide lubed fingers up our asses, gently teasing our prostates as they forced one, two, then three fingers inside our manholes. They finger fucked us as they bathed our balls with their tongues. Those sensations along with sucking my boyfriend's cock were proving to be a mighty powerful experience, to say the least. I felt Sean pull my ass cheeks apart. Allison's finger left my hole only to be replaced with Sean's thick meaty one. I was steadily devouring Sean's cock when I felt a new sensation along with some light giggling.

"Holy crap," I whispered. Watching the girls fucking like that was pretty hot, I had to admit. The only thing I wanted though was my dick inside Sean's ass. I was already hard and I pushed his head down to suck my dick briefly before I climbed behind him and slammed my cock balls deep into his hole.

"Ow, fuck me, Dylan. Take it easy."

But I was in no mood to take it easy. I began to plow him like a bitch and in moments, I had his face turned around and was kissing him deeply as the girls continued to fuck one another with the dildos shouting at me to 'Fuck that boy like a whore." I pulled Sean's ass apart and felt my balls slap him again and again as I bred him like a mare. Sweat dripped from my chest and face, falling in droplets on his furry, freckled back. I closed my eyes and reveled in the tightness of his manhole and the feel of his ass, the smell of his sweat and musk, and the tightness in my balls. I felt Allison's hands on my face. I opened my eyes.

"Fuck me," she whispered. "Fuck me like you are fucking your boyfriend. I want to know what that's like."

"I don't know if I can."

"Just try, Dylan," she said getting on all fours beside Sean.

Her pussy was open and pink and at that moment, I had to admit. I wanted to know what it was like. I pulled out of Sean's ass. She handed me a soapy washcloth and I quickly cleaned my penis. Her head was down, her cunt presented to me like a mandrill in heat. I gripped my cock and laid it against the lips of her pussy and pushed forward. The fleshy folds enveloped my penis like a velvet glove and I slid inside the warm, wet tunnel. Allison cried out in ecstasy. I gripped her waist and drove my cock in and out. The sensation was utterly foreign but my dick enjoyed the wetness and slick interior of the vagina since I was already so turned on. I looked across and Emily climbed onto Sean's belly and lowered her pussy onto his stiff pole. He looked at me with a crazed, maniacal look but reached up and gripped her tits and began to pump his cock in and out of her. I stared at his bull balls rolling around in his big sack as he thrust in and out of her cunt. His balls were a blur as he pummeled her pussy, her boobs shook and bounced. Her cries were high pitched and annoying, but the look of Sean's cock plowing her was transfixing. I felt my orgasm build again. I watched as Sean picked up his phone and pointed it at me. I smiled and reached down and grabbed mine. I slid the phone open and zoomed in on Sean's cock sliding in and out of Emily. Then pulled back and showed Sean gripping the girl's tits as he grinned at the camera. I shot the video down at my own dick sliding in and out of Allison's pussy, rotating the camera around to my own face, giving a big thumb's up. For some reason, the camera was the last straw and I felt my load building.

"I'm gonna cum," I groaned trying to pull out to shoot on Allison's ass.

"No! Cum in me. It's safe," she gasped.

I closed my eyes and felt my climax spurt deep within her as she screamed in orgasm herself. The walls of her vagina gripped my shaft like a vice as she came. I looked over hearing Sean growl. He slammed up hard into Emily's cunt. As his cock slid out, thick white ropes of semen dripped from her spent pussy.

Ten minutes later, we all sat naked in a hot Jacuzzi of bubbles, looking out at the mountains. I had one arm around Allison and the other around Sean. I took turns kissing each one of them. I even kissed Emily a few times. Allison got hot and sat on the edge of the tub. Emily moved between her legs and slid her tongue inside Allison's pink lips.

"You want to try some of this?" Emily asked. Sean and I both shook our heads. Fucking a hot pussy was one thing. Eating a dripping cunt was another. I wanted nothing to do with that. Instead, I floated over and sat in Sean's lap, kissing him deeply and soon his cock was sliding up inside my ass. He pulled me out of the water and I bent over as he reamed my ass hard and long. The girls fingered one another's pussy while they watched us fuck, sighing in deep gasps as they came along with us a few minutes later.

"I love watching you boys fuck," Allison said later as we all lay in a heap on the bed. "So was that the first time you ever…"

I grinned. "Was it that obvious?"

"No. You fucked like a pro, Dylan. Any girl would love to be mounted like that," she said. "So, any new revelations?"

I shrugged my shoulders. "Not really. It felt nice, sliding inside you and all that. I liked it. But at the end of the day, I think it only worked cause Sean was here and I was watching his dick and all that."

Allison smiled and kissed me sweetly. "Well, you can sure tell these motherfuckers that you had some pussy tonight – and it won't even be a lie. Use the video. Show them. Get out of here and go get married or something," she said. "But let's make a pact."

"Oh?" I asked.

"If none of us are married in a few years, let's get back together and just be one big group. Our own version of Big Love. You boys can keep fucking and we can watch and help and who knows, maybe we can have a bunch of kids and make a big family out of it."

Sean and I laughed. I could tell Allison was serious though. I leaned over and kissed her. "Okay, that sounds pretty great actually. What about it, brother?"

"I like the idea of having girls around to make babies and dinner," he said with a smirk. Emily slapped him on the shoulder.

"You dick," she said hugging him close.

"Even if you boys stay together," Allison said. "If Em and I aren't married, maybe we can get together and make those babies?"

We all hugged tight. My cock swelled and soon it was sliding inside Allison's pussy as I doggie-styled her deep while leaning over and kissing Sean while he fucked Emily.

He grinned. "This is so fucked up. But damn, it's kind of fun too."

We left the girls' room around 3:00 am and made our way back to our quad. We peeked into Manny's room and saw JaMarcus's dark ass sticking out from under the sheet. His heavy arm was draped over Manny's belly. We went into my bedroom and pulled off our clothes. I grabbed my phone and pulled up the videos of me and Sean fucking the girls and sent it to Saul's cell phone with a big smiley face emoticon. Sean smiled and gave me a fist-bump and squeezed my sack. We climbed into my bed and I pulled Sean close. My hand held his cock that was hard once again, sticky precum slick against my thumb.

"I did not expect that tonight," I said.

"That makes two of us."

"What did you think?"

Sean's blue-green eyes sparkled in the dim light. I thought he might actually be crying a bit. I held him close. Soon warm salty tears flowed from my eyes too. I climbed on top of him and rubbed my erection against him as we held one another.

"What's wrong, baby?" I asked rubbing his tears from his cheeks.

"I don't know. I guess part of me kind of wishes I was just normal. You know, wanting just pussy and all that. Would be so simple."

"I know. Only one problem with that really," I said.

Sean looked at me for an answer.

"I'd have to give this up." I said. "I don't want to. What's wrong with us finding each other, falling in love, and spending the rest of our lives together? I don't give a shit what my mom says. I don't care what bullshit these idiots spread either. I have always wanted to fall in love and now, I have. They don't get to dictate how that happens. So many kids we went to school with had moms and dads that couldn't stand one another. Half the dads were out there fucking around and some of the moms too. How is that better than you and me? They can all go to hell if they want to judge me. Kissing you, sucking your dick, sliding my cock inside you or riding your pecker, that's the best I have ever felt and I never want to quit. I won't quit. I love cock and I will until I die." I could feel my heart beating hard in my chest. Sean grinned and held me tight.

"Don't hold back, brother. Tell me what you really think," he said sliding his fingers into the crack of my ass. "I fit inside your pussy better than anywhere else. I want you to be my husband. I want to marry you and have some little boys of our own and be a family. My parents can either get on board, or they can get left behind."

I reached behind my ass and gripped Sean's penis and guided it into my hole. He was thick and hard and it hurt, it hurt like the most wonderful hurt in the whole world and we fell asleep with his cock deep inside.

Chapter 7
Come on in, Take a Seat

My phone chirped around 7:30 AM the next morning. I leaned over and held the screen up to see a text from Saul.

Touchdown, brothers. Come see me this morning after breakfast.

"Figures that would get his attention," Sean rumbled in his early morning low voice. He slid down in the bed and pulled my ass apart and began to push his tongue deep into my hole. I spread my legs wide apart and gripped his head and pressed his face tight against my crack. He pulled my asshole apart and drilled his tongue in deep, sliding a finger and then two down inside. He spun around and gripped my ankles and pushed my legs up toward my head and I felt the wet tip of his dick touch my rosebud. He pushed forward and penetrated me in one slow slide until his shaft filled me, his sack pressed hard against my ass. He pulled almost all the way out and then drove in again to the hilt. I groaned as his thick seven inches split me open in a torrent of heavy thrusts. I tried to catch my breath but the crazy Irishman didn't let up. He fucked like a crazy man, breeding me deep, filling my ass with a fat morning load of his spunk.

We lay there in a heap afterwards, his seed slowly leaking from my spent hole when a naked Manny and JaMarcus walked in. Their penises were hard and I had a distinct feeling they had woken up and started playing very much like Sean and I had done. JaMarcus pushed my legs apart and touched the pearly white sperm leaking from my hole. He smiled and pointed to Manny. The married man scooted forward on the bed and aimed his erection at my used hole and pressed his cock inside with a loud grunt.

"Fuck, I love sloppy seconds," he said as he filled my ass with his cock.

JaMarcus pushed Sean's legs apart and began to munch on his red furry hole. Sean held his ankles to keep his legs apart as the man licked and tongued his hole, moving up to Sean's sack and cock then returning to his hole, pulling the fleshy knot far apart. JaMarcus moved up in-between Sean's legs and spit a thick drop of saliva onto the big round head of his cock and fitted it into Sean's anus and pushed hard. Sean's head slid back as he groaned and pulled his legs apart so JaMarcus's thick penis could slide all eight inches deep inside his hole. Soon, the room was filled with slapping bellies, sweaty balls, and pounding cock along with the musky smell of used ass. Manny and JaMarcus continued to thrust and drill inside our manholes until they shot their morning load deep into our asses. The men kissed long and hard. Manny's thick black goatee brushed against my lips and face as he kissed and continued to slide his thick cock in and out of my ass. I gripped his firm, furry ass and pulled him deep inside. I saw out of my peripheral vision, JaMarcus and Sean kissing deeply as the black man slowly drove his dick in and out of Sean's spent hole.

We lay all together in the bed afterward, enjoying the early morning sun playing across our naked bodies as it streamed in the open window. Manny's kisses continued and I had to admit, he was fucking sexy as shit. No wonder the guy was like cock kryptonite to so many young guys like me. His furry chest and belly rubbed gently against me as we kissed. All I wanted to do was return the favor and fuck his beautiful married ass.

"So, you guys left with those girls last night," JaMarcus said rubbing Sean's furry belly and playing with his soft cock. "Y'all get some pussy?"

Sean looked over at me and grinned. He stretched across and grabbed my phone and opened the videos and pressed play, holding the screen up for Manny and JaMarcus to see.

"No fucking way," Manny said staring at the phone. "Holy shit, you boys really did fuck those girls."

"Sure did."

"What was that shit like?" JaMarcus said looking at the video.

I shrugged. "It was good. I mean they were very cool. They mostly wanted to watch us fuck each other."

"Except for when they were fucking us up the ass with those strap-ons"

"Bullshit. They did not."

Sean laughed. "They sure did. Opened my ass up good. I got so turned on watching Allison fuck Dylan that I slid my cock inside Emily's pussy. Felt pretty good as long as I was watching her work on this guy's asshole."

"Did you wear a rubber?" Manny said rolling the video once again.

Sean and I looked at one another. "Um, no. They said it was safe."

JaMarcus and Manny burst out laughing. "What a couple of rubes," Manny said. "Of course no girl ever lied about that before. You idiots might have just impregnated a couple of skanks."

My mind felt like it had snapped. Somehow in the back of my mind, I knew the guys were right and the idea of being so careless and stupid made my face glow red. I looked over at Sean who was sitting with a blank look on his face, clearly digesting this information.

"Did you fools actually shoot your nut up in that nasty pussy?" JaMarcus said. "Damn, you guys are too stupid for words."

I spoke up, though not with great confidence. "I don't think those girls were looking for a baby daddy. I'm pretty sure they are on the pill or have an IUD or something."

"But you don't know, Einstein," Manny said. "That's just how I got my third kid."

"Besides that, you don't know what kind of STDs those girls might have," JaMarcus said.

"Well for that matter, you don't know what kind we might have either. Or you have," Sean said with some heat in his voice.

That comment seemed to sober the four of them to the point of distraction. Manny got up and left the room, heading to the bathroom. I followed him inside and climbed into the shower with him. I grabbed a bar of soap and ran it over his back and ass. He turned around and soaped up my chest and my cock. We kissed and groped one another. My finger slid deep inside Manny's furry hole. He spread his legs apart and my finger slid deeper inside. The door to the bathroom opened and Sean stood looking into the shower. He looked a little pissed to say the least.

"There's more room in here," Manny said. "Come join us. Your boyfriend here is working on my hole pretty good."

Sean slid into the tiled shower. His hand joined mine and we both fingered Manny's hole. He joined me in kissing the man, our tongues teasing and licking each other. I dropped to my knees and took Manny's thick penis into my mouth. Sean moved around and fit his cock into Manny's ass and pushed forward with a loud grunt. Manny swore and spread his legs as Sean began to fuck him violently. In moments, my mouth was filled with sour, spicy semen. I stood up and we continued to wash one another.

"Where's JaMarcus?" I asked.

Sean rubbed the soap into his crack and washed his ass. "Ed, one of the directors, called on the intercom and asked him to head over to his office early."

"That's weird," I said. For some reason I had a really funny feeling. Actually, my stomach clinched tight along with my sphincter. Something just didn't feel right. "Why would he be calling?" Manny slid his arm around me and turned me to the wall. *Fuck, did this guy ever run out of nut,* I wondered? He pushed his cock inside my asshole. His strong arms held me tight to the wall, my butt stuck out as he plowed my furry trench. Sean stooped down and took my cock into his mouth again. Manny hissed a string of raunchy, filthy words into my ear as he bred me hard and long. It was almost like getting fucked by my mentor dad. He was so dominant and mature. His seed blasted into my ass as I unloaded into Sean's. So much sperm this morning. I was loving it. I climbed out of the shower and dried off looking back at Sean and Manny kissing and groping one another still, fingering assholes and stroking one another's cocks.

My phone buzzed and I looked at the screen. It was a text from Saul.

> *Don't forget to come see me after breakfast.* I texted back.
> *I will. BTW, why did Bro. Ed need to see JaMarcus so early this AM?*
> *What? I don't know. I'll find out. L8ter.*

That bit of info didn't do much to make me feel better. I went to my room and pulled on a pair of New Balance boxer briefs. Sean walked in drying off his sack and butt.

"Did you finally get enough cum for breakfast?" I said like a bitch. His eyebrows rose up and I'm pretty sure he was going to say something snarky when a voice sounded over the intercom.

"Good morning brothers. Sean, can you and Manny please come by the director's office on your way to breakfast this morning?"

Sean looked at me with a twinge of concern but walked to the speaker and pressed the button. "Sure. We'll be right there. Um, you want Dylan to come too?"

"No. Just the two of you, thanks," the voice answered pleasant and musical.

Sean bent over and stepped into his Polo briefs and pulled them up over his big ass. "That's weird. Why does that make me feel fucking nervous?"

"I don't know. Same for me. Something is up. While you go find out, I'm going to go find Saul and see if he knows anything. Keep your phone handy. I'll text you if I can to let you know."

Manny walked into the room, naked and pale, holding his underwear and shorts. "What the fuck, homes?" Why you think we need to go see the director?"

"Hell if I know. Maybe it's just one of those routine kinds of interviews and all that. Shit, I mean, I fucked a girl so he can't be too mad at me."

"Well, I've fucked one for fifteen years, plus all the ones before her, and I'm still here," Manny said pulling on his shorts. "This is making me really freaked out."

I laid a hand on his strong shoulder. "It's okay, hermano. I'll go see Saul and see if I can find anything out. It's going to be fine."

Sean and Manny pulled on t-shirts and flip-flops and headed off to the director's office. I finished dressing and took off for the main building where Saul's office was located. My stomach was growling and my ass felt weird, like I was ready to have a huge diarrhea explosion. *Fuck, I shouldn't have had all that butt sex today*, I thought to myself. I bounded up the stairs to the main building, turning toward the administrative offices instead of the cafeteria. My belly lurched at the smells of bacon and toast coming from the lunch room. I wandered around the halls and came to Saul's office. He was talking on the phone and did not look happy. He motioned me in. I sat down and felt my stomach do another cartwheel. Saul hung up and rubbed his eyes.

"Hey, Dylan. Thanks for coming over. You had quite a night, I guess. Congratulations on consummating intercourse with that young lady. I hope you enjoyed yourself."

I stared at him incomprehensive. "Uh, yeah. I mean, it was pretty strange and all that. But, my dick did the trick and I have to say it was fun," I added not completely truthfully.

Saul smiled weakly and moved around to the front of his desk to stand in front of me.

"I need to ask you something. Did you guys come home last night and fuck around together?

"What?" I said in fake shock.

Saul gripped my shoulders and stared at me in true hopelessness. "Did you guys fuck each other last night, or this morning? Did you? Tell me, Dylan. Don't lie."

I pulled away from him, or at least tried to. His big meaty hands held me in place. His face was close to mine and I could feel his warm breath on my cheeks. I stared at him in terror wondering if he was about to slap the shit out of me. I gulped.

"Okay, yeah. I mean, we did. We didn't mean to. It just happened."

Saul's eyes closed and he lowered his head in defeat. "Oh God, Dylan."

"What? Look, I know we've been breaking a few rules. It's hard to quit, you know. We don't mean to. It's just really tough when we live together and really like one another and all that." Now I began to really panic. "We'll stop. Okay? I mean it, we will just follow the rules and try really hard to just like girls and…"

Saul looked up at me. There were tears in the corner of his eyes. He lowered his head and touched it to my forehead. His hands were trembling. I reached up and gripped his hands and pulled them off my shoulders and stared at him.

"What is it, Saul? Does it have something to do with the director calling for all of us? I mean everyone besides me? Tell me."

"They've been watching all you guys. They forbid me to tell you. There are cameras in everyone's quad. They have been spending time with a few of the other quads. The guys in quad seven were sneaking into each other's beds. I guess they must have finally gotten around to watching the footage from your quad."

All of the blood drained from my face. "You've seen us? You've been watching us?

A tear fell from Saul's eye onto his navy blue shirt. "I've been watching from the first. I've hardly been doing anything else. I watch you guys fuck and sit in here and jack off all the time. I tried to deflect them toward the other quads. Shit, almost all the guys here fuck around a little. But goddamn, you boys are setting a new record. I've never seen guys suck and fuck as much as you. It's like this sweet torture all the time. I can't quit watching. I've deleted some of the footage so they wouldn't see but not last night's. I actually had a damn date with my girlfriend. I get the idea you guys had a marathon fuck fest. Tell me you didn't."

I stared in horror. My mouth went totally dry and I started to fall out of the chair. Saul's face contorted and he shook his head in solemn realization. "Oh holy shit," he whispered.

"What are they going to do?"

Saul's eyes opened in fury. "They are going to put all of you in the fucking chair and try and reprogram your ass." Saul's phone chirped. He looked at the screen. "Fuck."

"What is it?"

"They want me to go find you and bring you to the director's office. Oh holy fuck."

"Don't do it," I pleaded. "Please, I will promise not to fool around anymore. Please, Saul, just don't let them…"

He looked at me in utter dismay. "I don't have a choice. I have to take you. I'm really sorry, Dylan. I like all of you guys so much. Look, I've been in the chair. It's bad, but you will do fine and it will help you not like dick so much after they get through with you."

"Saul," I cried, tears flowed from my eyes. "Please don't do it. Save me. Save all of us."

"I can't. They know you are here. I will try and think of something. But you have to come with me now or they will come drag you there. I promise, I will try and make them reconsider. Trust me."

My mind was in neutral. I felt hollow and incapable of any action or thought. Saul pulled me to my feet and wrapped his arms around me. He pulled me close, his hands rubbing my back and sliding down to my ass and gripping me tight. His dick pressed into my belly, hard and rigid. His face was close. I felt his lips close on mine and I opened my mouth to his hungry kiss. His tongue slid inside my mouth. He broke off the kiss.

"What the fuck is wrong with me?" he hissed. "I'm cured of that shit!" His erection pressing into my belly dared to object with that sentiment. He wrapped a strong arm around my shoulders and began to lead me toward the director's office. Part of me wanted to push back and run away. Another part was just so weary of the whole stupid place, I was ready to strap myself in the fucking chair if it could just get me out of here and back home. I wouldn't mind just falling in love with a girl and getting married and all that. But it was going to take giving me a new brain, because my current one just didn't think like that at all.

Saul pushed me through a series of doors and corridors and soon I was ushered into a dark, eerie room that pulsed with unknown energy and malevolence. The light was so dim, I couldn't make anything out other than it appeared there were some sort of large recliners in a row facing a movie screen. Saul was pushed away while large hands from the shadows gripped me. Rough hands gripped me and began pulling at my clothes. Soon I was naked and pushed back into the recliner chair. My head was strapped against a head rest. My chest was strapped to the back of the chair. My arms and hands were restrained as were my legs. My mouth was forced open and a ball gag was fitted inside. A wire contraption was fitted to my face that gripped my eyelids and forced them open so I couldn't blink. I began to struggle and pull against the restraints, my nerves taking over and making me fight the bonds. But there was no getting loose. Hands gripped my penis and pulled it roughly up and wrapped coils around it and fitted something into the piss slit in my dick that burned like fire. My balls were wrapped in some sort of tight apparatus that spread them apart, holding each orb in a web of wires. I realized the recliner chair had a hole in the seat. I felt a whirring sensation against my anus and realized a thick probe of some kind was slowly penetrating my ass like an alien cock. I screamed and pulled against the mechanism but to no avail. I felt the probe push like Sean's dick further and further inside me and press against my prostate. My asshole quivered and trembled. Some vibration began in the probe and my cock responded and filled with blood, the cage of wires covering it digging into the flesh. My balls were forced even further apart and the probe fucked even deeper inside me. I yelled into the gag but no more than guttural groans came out. The lights in the room dimmed even more and the screen began to glow. I turned my head slightly to the right and saw Sean in the chair beside me, restrained and probed like I was. He looked at me with wild eyes that were dry and frozen in place like mine. His cock stuck straight up, his big balls like plums pressed hard against the skin of his scrotum.

To my left, Manny was locked in place. His face looked swollen like he had been punched in the eyes or jaw. His erection was steadily leaking precum and his big brown balls were swollen and tight in his furry black sack. I saw the probe moving up and down in his anus as he squirmed. He looked at me in fear and horror. Beyond him, JaMarcus was in the shadows and the only thing I could make out were the whites of his eyes and the glistening tip of his penis that must be leaking fluid like the rest of us. A voice came through the headphones that had been placed on my ears.

"Brothers. Sadly, other behavior modification efforts with you have proven ineffective to retrain your minds and actions from the perversions of a homosexual lifestyle. You have continued to sodomize one another and act shamefully and sinfully. This cannot be tolerated. Today, we begin your reprogramming in earnest. This device will reward your mind and body as it responds positively to heterosexual images of intercourse and foreplay. Similarly, you will be punished when your body responds with arousal to homosexual images, queer love, and filthy oral and anal sex with other men. If your body does not comply, you will suffer some pain and discomfort. Conversely, as your body responds in arousal to godly heterosexual images, you will be rewarded with pleasure and orgasms. These apparatuses will allow you to have many more orgasms that your body would normally be capable of. This session will take some time. There will be no stopping. If your body needs to eliminate waste, you will simply have to foul yourself and be cleaned up afterwards. Prepare yourselves, gentlemen. You are in for a hell of a ride."

My heart was beating so loud in my ears, I thought my head was in a bass drum. The video began. Beautiful scenes of sunsets, rainbows, and the ocean filled the screen. The probe in my ass thrummed with a vibration that tickled my prostate and made my cock swell with blood. My balls felt tight and tingling. Next, there were horrible images of dead animals, blood, car accidents, and even a beheading. There was no way to turn away from the screen. The probe fucked hard and painfully into my ass. My balls felt lightly shocked and smarted from the current that arced along the wires.

The screen filled with a young college aged girl masturbating, the camera going in for a close up on the frilly internal labia that fell from her vagina like tiny curtains. My penis deflated like a leaky balloon. The more the girl fondled her clit, the more I wanted to be sick. Then the screen filled with a buff football player with a lightly furry ass being pushed apart and licked by an older football coach looking man. The older man ate the boy's ass and fingered his hole then sucked the massive penis that fell between the boy's legs before the man entered him and began to fuck in wild abandon. My cock swelled and pressed hard against the cage surrounding it. Suddenly, the probe in my ass began to pulse and shock me causing waves of nausea. My penis was squeezed. My balls were shocked and felt like tiny nails were being dug into the sensitive flesh. The tip of my cock was probed then squeezed. My nipples burned like fire from the strap around my chest. This continued incessantly until the image changed to a young college girl being anally penetrated by someone who looked old enough to be a father. Although this was a total disgusting turn-off to me in every way, the vibrations in my ass and the rhythmic stimulation of my penis made me grow hard and harder until I groaned and my semen spurted from my cock in thick white ropes. The other guys must have been feeling the same as I saw silvery ribbons launch from their chairs toward the screen. My eyes burned from being held open by the thin metal contraption around my head. I heard Sean sobbing beside me. Before I could catch my breath, the images began again, beautiful, sickly horrible, men fucking girls or women or women blowing big dicks and then the images of guys sucking or kissing or fucking. The minute those images appeared which were certain to get our dicks at least a little chubbed, the pain seared through our balls, ass, and cocks. My body felt like it was on fire. Then the guys would return to fucking strange plucked pussies and the pleasurable vibrations and sensations would build until we were cumming again.

I heard Manny groan and I turned my head to see his face in a rictus of pain. He shouted and a shower of piss splattered from his cock on his belly and legs. The plug in my ass continued to drill and plow endlessly inside my rectum. I wondered how much more I could take before my bowels surrendered and poured from my ruined manhole. I looked over on the other side of Sean. Brother Ed was standing at a podium of controls with dials and gauges and spinning lights. It reminded me of the "Dagger of the Mind" episode of Star Trek when Captain Kirk was being subjected to the mind-control of the neural neutralizer. Brother Ed was pressing buttons and dials. I could also see his pants were bunched around his ankles. The fucker was masturbating while torturing all of us like some goddamn Dick Cheney. I saw others just beyond the lights. I couldn't make out their faces, but the silvery light illuminated their hands and bare legs and fat cocks that were being stroked in the shadows of the oscillating images. I couldn't help but notice, they stroked just as happily or maybe more when the guys were on screen than just the girls. Fucking hypocrites.

Our ears were filled with the breathless voice of the director again. "You fucking fags. Your dicks are still hard with the queers and limp as a noodle with the pussy. I'm gonna fry your brains if that's what it takes. Dirty homos. Guys like you turned me into a gay. Now I have to fight it all the time. I'll change your brains if it kills you!"

With that, Brother Ed pressed on buttons and turned the dials up to eleven. The images of young men being butt fucked by burly bears came on and the pain in our asses and balls exploded. The probes fucked us deep and painful like glass being shoved in our anuses. My chest burned and pounded. My cock felt like it was being pulled off my body. From the corner of my eye, I saw one of the shadowed men collapse to the floor. A moment later, another fell, his naked ass illuminated in the flashes of the movie screen, his cock rigid and leaking. There appeared to be some sort of scuffle and a loud shout and thud and another pantless form fell. The director turned and screamed.

"What the..! No, you fucking faggot!"

Suddenly, he flew across the floor. His hard cock flopped against his fat belly as he lay motionless in front of the screen. Hands flew over the dials and gauges and the pain and images stopped. My heart was racing. My ass felt like a truck had been driven through it as the probe flopped out. I was close to blacking out as the large form moved from the darkness to the dim light in front of me and reached for the restraints on my chest.

"Saul. I knew you would come."

"Don't talk, baby. Those motherfuckers." His large hands gripped my penis and extracted it from the wire cage. He released my testicles and then my arms and head. He eased the hooks holding my eyelids open from my eyes and I collapsed into his arms. His lips touched my forehead and then my lips. "I'm so sorry, buddy. So sorry." He laid me on the floor and went to help the others. Soon, all my quad brothers lay beside me, catching our breath and wincing from the pain in our genitals and ass.

"Do you feel like you can stand, guys?" Saul asked. "If you can, we need to get the fuck out of here."

I struggled to my feet and leaned over and helped Sean to his feet. He hugged me tightly and kissed the side of my face. I saw Manny and JaMarcus embracing as well. I turned to Saul and pulled him to me. I whispered into his ear. He smiled wickedly.

"Sounds like a plan to me," he answered.

Five minutes later, the five of us made our way out of the room. Brother Ed and the others were strapped and wired to the chairs, eyelids hooked wide open. Saul reversed the dials and turned the power all the way up. Collective groans filled the room as the pain makers worked their magic on their holes and cocks while images of girls and pussy filled the screen. As the movie changed to college jocks sucking cock and eating ass, the pleasure controls kicked in and the groans were replaced with moans as the men's erections grew and exploded in rivers of cum. Saul took the key and broke it off in the panel. No one was going to easily shut the fucking thing off any time soon. We found our clothes and pulled on what we could and ran from the room, locking the door behind us.

Ten minutes later, the four of us piled into one of the center's minivans and sped toward the Willamette Valley. As the pine trees and sagebrush sped by in a blur outside the windows of the vehicle, I leaned up and wrapped my arms around Saul who was driving. I planted a big kiss on the side of his face. He reached up and held my face close to his. I rubbed his big chest and let my hands slide down to his belly.

"Thank you for saving us, Saul. We all owe you our balls."

He grinned. "You bet your ass you do. And I intend to dump a load of my nut into every one of you as soon as I can."

"Brother Saul! Sounds like you might be having a relapse," Manny said patting the big man on the shoulder.

"Nah. My head is screwed on straight for the first time in months. I think girls are fine. I even might say I enjoy the occasional straight sex experience. But I live for cock. So sorry I played a part in all that guys."

All of us reached up and patted Saul letting him know there were no hard feelings. We sat quietly either holding hands or with our arms around each other, watching the dry high desert turn back into the verdant forests of the Pacific Northwest. After thirty miles or so, Saul pulled off on a forest road and after taking a few turns, was conveniently alone on an isolated logging landing, miles from the nearest person.

"I gotta piss, brothers." Saul said climbing out of the van. He walked to the edge of the landing and pulled out his penis, pushing his pants down to his ankles as he pissed. I pulled up beside him and followed suit. Soon, all five of us stood on the landing watering the trees far below, feeling the cool mountain air caress our sore asses. I heard a scraping of gravel and turned to see Manny and JaMarcus unrolling two sleeping bags on the hard ground. Manny pulled his shirt off and stepped out of his shorts. Soon, the rest of us were naked beside him. We stood with our hands on our hips as a naked, repentant Saul moved from dick to dick, sucking us deep and long and lapping our precum that leaked from our tired cocks. Sean moved behind Saul and pulled his heavy, meaty ass apart and drove his tongue deep inside. I sunk to my knees and let his thick eight inch penis fill my mouth. Manny bathed his balls with his tongue as JaMarcus fed the big man his cock. With a loud grunt, Sean penetrated Saul's ass and drove his cock balls deep inside the fuzzy manhole. Saul moaned as he was ridden by Sean, reaching around to pull Sean's dick deeper and deeper into his anus. Sean shuddered and unloaded his semen into Saul's hole and stepped back. I aimed my cock at Saul's dripping hole and slid inside. The warmth of Saul's rectum with Sean's jizz lubing my shaft made me more aroused than ever. I came in huge blasts of nut until the white cream leaked from the edges of Saul's hole. I pulled off and Manny took my place. His tanned cock plowing deep and hard inside the man's cunt. Saul gripped the back of his legs and took Manny's cock slamming against his taint until the man shouted and sprayed a thick fountain of salsa deep inside his pussy. JaMarcus's eight inches spread Saul's asshole wide and the men groaned in unison. JaMarcus's sack slammed again and again against Saul's low hangers until the black man's seed erupted in a huge fountain of white inside Saul's gaping hole. JaMarcus pulled out and a torrent of sperm flowed from Saul's open ass and coated his furry balls. The men pulled together in a tight circle and kissed and licked one another's lips and faces until they were wet and dripping.

"I love you all so much," Saul said. "Thanks for saving me too."

Sean held up his fist and bumped Saul's large mitt. "Bros before Hos every time, my friend."

We got our clothes back on and headed back down the mountains toward our homes. I was nervous but felt like my life was finally on track. I hoped my mom would be glad to see me again. But if not, then I was okay wishing her well and going on my own way. I slid my hand into Sean's and laid my head on his big shoulder.

"You know," I said to the group, "I didn't really have a clear idea when I got sent to Straight Ahead. But one thing's for certain now."

"What's that?" Sean asked.

"Conversion therapy made me gay for sure."

The van roared with laughter and Saul punched the satellite radio and blasted Maroon 5's "Animal" from the speakers as we made our way down the mountain.

Chapter 8
Happily Ever After – Five Years Later

I rolled over and felt Sean's arms slide around me. His morning erection slid between my ass cheeks and teased my hole. I smiled and gripped my leg and lifted my knee up as he spit into his hand and lubed his shaft. He slid easily inside my ass, smashing his balls against my ass. I sucked in my breath as he set up a quick rhythmic pounding, his belly smacking my ass and making tiny sucking sounds as his penis plowed deep into my ass.

"God, I love fucking you, Baby," he growled in his low early morning voice. I reached behind him and pulled his big ass deeper and deeper into me. His breath hissed into my air as he unloaded his morning nut into my bowels. As his penis slid from my ass, he pulled me over and swallowed my erection and sucked my cock until I flooded his mouth with semen.

He kissed me with cummy breath, his tongue sliding inside my mouth. "I love you too, husband." I gripped his face, our fingers were entwined, our wedding bands lightly clinking as we gripped hands. "We need to get up, though. We need to get on the road early."

"When are we supposed to be at your folks?"

"Around 1:00. Mom has it all planned out so we don't want to be late."

The door to the bedroom burst open and two small blurs hopped onto the bed and tackled us. "Yaah, we're being attacked," Sean yelled in surprise. "How's Sam doing this morning and his sidekick, Angus?

"Come on, Daddy. We are supposed to get up early," Sam answered, the small black haired boy giggling as Sean held him down and blew a loud raspberry on his belly below his navel.

"You too, Papa," Angus admonished me before dissolving into squeals of laughter as I tickled his belly and under his chin, rubbing his red hair into a crazy haystack of curls. The almost five-year-old boys giggled and climbed under the covers and snuggled against us.

"Your bed smells funny, like fish sticks," the blond boy said putting his head under the covers.

"And you forgot to wear your pajamas again," the red-haired boy said. "I can see your penis."

"Yeah, well. We see yours all the time too." Sean said tickling both the boys again. "Why don't you monkeys go get some bowls and cereal and we will come pour the milk for you in just a minute?"

"Race you," Sam said leaping from the bed with Angus giggling after him. Their underoos-clad bottoms bounding down the hall. Sean leaned over to me and sniffed near my crotch. "You do smell like fish sticks…and bleach."

"Shut up, you dick," I said. I pulled on some underwear and headed down the hall to the kitchen. The boys were at the table with cereal poured in their bowls and quite a bit on the table as well. I grabbed the milk and poured it on the cereal and kissed both of them on the top of the head. "Daddy and I are going to jump in the shower. Will you be good and careful?"

"Yes Papa," they both said with mouths full of Cheerios.

I went back to the bedroom and slid my shorts off and opened the glass door and slid my arms around Sean. My hands found his penis and balls and began to soap them up with the shower gel I poured in my palm. Soon we were soapy and hard again. Sean groaned as I penetrated his rosebud. He gripped the wall and took my hard fucks like a pro, our bodies slapping and sliding against each other. I pushed hard and deep inside his hole.

"Fuck, take it easy, husband. I swear to fuck your cock is still growing. That big boy is banging on my prostate like a jackhammer."

"Just like you like it."

"You know it. Shit, I'm gonna cum," Sean said, thick white sperm leaking from his erection.

I grunted loud and unloaded my nuts into his ass. "God I love you so much. We better get out of here before the boys see us fucking again."

"I know. They aren't going to buy the leap frog bullshit for much longer," Sean said.

Later, I reached over and held Sean's hand as we drove toward Sheridan. My thumb rubbed the fine red hairs that covered the back of his hand. He looked over at me and smiled. The sun was out and warm. His big muscled legs strained against the cargo shorts he wore. The outline of his dick was prominent in the big pouch that filled the crotch of his shorts. I rubbed the mushroom head lightly and he grinned bigger, looking into the backseat to watch the boys staring out at the landscape outside.

"Watch it, Mister," he whispered. "I'll have to pull over and take you into the bushes to pee."

"Nah, the monkeys would just want to pee with us. You know how they are." The fact was, the boys typically went outside to pee in the yard even when the bathroom was totally free. The joys of being a boy. "They will be watering my mom's petunias this weekend if we aren't careful."

"Your dad would just laugh about it. I swear he's the one that taught them how to piss on a tree so good. Every time I am out in the yard with him talking, he hauls out his dong and takes a big piss."

"What's a dong?" Sam asked from the back seat.

"Um. You heard that, huh, Super Ears??

"We both did. What's a dong?" Angus asked.

"It's just another word for penis," I said trying to be nonchalant.

The boys dissolved into giggles and Sam reached over and playfully racked his brother in the balls with his fist. "Got your dong," he said. Angus instantly reached over and punched Sam in the nuts.

"I dinged your dong too."

"Thanks a lot," I said. "Okay fellows. I know that's funny but please, don't be saying that around your grandparents or your friends or teachers. Just around us, understand?"

"Sure thing, Daddy Dong," Sam said giggling even more.

"Christ," Sean hissed. I elbowed him hard.

"Knock that shit off."

"Papa said the S-word," Angus said.

I bit my lip and closed my eyes. Sean laughed like a maniac. He pulled off to a rest area. "Let's let these monkeys out to drain their dongs and get some energy out." The boys shrieked in laughter.

We sat on a picnic table watching the boys run around. Sean draped his arm around me. "You know how lucky we are?"

"I do. I'm grateful every single day. That reminds me, Allison called and said she and Emily are hoping to come out here in July. The girls are old enough now to make the trip easier. It will be good to see them again for sure. It's been almost a year."

"I know the boys will be over the moon. They love when the moms come around. Will be good to see our girls too. I don't like them being so far away."

"I know, but that's where their jobs took them. We better load up."

We drove up I-5 watching the hills fly by. Sean had the video going in the back seat. The boys were watching "Up" for the hundredth time. I leaned my head against the window and closed my eyes. So many thoughts were in my mind. My mind drifted back to five years ago. Sean and I pulled up at my home, our hearts in our throats. We had only vaguely described our ordeal at the center to our families. As we walked into the house, my mother had literally flown at me, wrapping me in her arms, sobbing uncontrollably. She had pleaded with us to forgive her for sending us to what she described as a concentration camp. My dad held me for so long, weeping along with my mom. They had welcomed Sean like another son, showering him with hugs and kisses as well. My dad was even so bold when we were alone in the back yard to tell me Sean was quite a "hottie" and wondered if the fat basket in Sean's pants was as impressive when he was naked, patting me on the ass and kissing my cheek. I never got the whole story of what happened that turned my mom around, but it seemed to have something to do with a very real and scary dream she had where Jesus himself had looked at her with tears in his eyes and simply said…"I gave that boy to you and you just threw him out. He's perfect, just like he is." It had shaken her to the core and she was a totally reformed person, even going so far as becoming politically active in Pro-LGBT rallies and bringing marriage equality to Oregon.

As if that wasn't enough, a few months later, Allison and Emily showed up with an intriguing proposal, soon after Sean and I got married. They proposed to be surrogate moms for us if we would be the sperm donors for them on with their second pregnancy. They were free spirit girls, enjoying the company of boyfriends from time to time, but feeling like the two of them were more a family than getting married to men. Somehow, we got our heads around it and a year later, the two of them gave birth to healthy boys. Sean and I had taken turns fucking both of the girls, deciding we would let the universe sort out who would be the dad with who. As it turned out, Emily and I conceived little Super Mario Sam, while Allison gave birth to our redheaded Angus. Two years later, we had a month of fucking with the girls again and this time, I knocked up Allison and Sean and Emily made a baby. Both were girls this time, one blonde beauty and my little brunette doll. It was strange to not see the girls all the time, but we knew the girls missed our boys the same way. But at the end of the day, our kids had parents and even more than one set, it seemed. Sean and I both had great jobs, the boys were so happy with us, and loved when they got to see their moms. They never complained about them not being around all the time. To them, it was just how it was. And my mom (and Sean's for that matter) were more than adequate female role models for the boys. We saw the grandparents all the time. My dad was crazy for the boys, building them a fort in the backyard, taking them fishing, and skinny-dipping together in the swimming hole on the river behind their house. Watching my boys cavort with my dad in the water was like a healing balm. Sean and I would hang back and watch them play together, soaking naked in the water ourselves. I smiled thinking of watching my dad's eyes widen as he saw Sean's big naked ass or low hanging balls swing as he walked along the river bank. My mom didn't balk at the unconventional birth arrangement either, just being so grateful that she had four grandbabies to spoil, even if she didn't get to see the girls that much.

My phone chirped and I roused. I looked at the screen and smiled as I saw a selfie photo of Saul and JaMarcus with Manny's wide grin right in the middle. The phone chirped again and this time, it was a close up of Manny's face with two big dicks sliding into his mouth from both sides. I carefully showed Sean whose eyes popped open and he gripped his dick and bit his lip mouthing, 'Damn' as he stroked his penis through his pants.

"They having a get-together weekend?" Sean asked looking at the cock pic again.

"Guess so. Manny's wife must have let him out for the weekend."

In an interesting turn of events, Saul and JaMarcus had eventually fallen in love and gotten married last summer. They lived near Manny and spent a good bit of time with Manny and his family. They had gotten to know Maricella, Manny's wife and she seemed to genuinely care for them as well. She had even made the remarkable concession that as long as he stuck with Saul or JaMarcus (and interestingly me and Sean as well.) she was fine with his having playtime with the boys, as long as he came back home to her. It was a perfect arrangement for Manny who had no desire to run away from his family. He just loved penis as well as his wife and kids. So, our strange collaborative families continued to grow and love one another.

We were nearing the exit to Salem when Sean turned to me. "Were you thinking about Saul and everyone?"

"Yeah. Were you?"

"Yeah. I would like to see them." Sean leaned close and whispered. "And fuck the shit out of all of them." He looked in the backseat. "Up!" still held the boys' attention.

"That makes two of us."

"You know," Sean began. "We owe that f-ing Straight Ahead place a lot. Without it, I might never have met you. We wouldn't have our boys and girls. And we wouldn't have our great buddies. In a funny way, that shit-hole place gave us the families we always dreamed of."

I squeezed Sean's hand and leaned over and kissed him.

"You said the S-word again," Sam said with a giggle.

~~The End~~

Here is a sample from another story you may enjoy:

Here Comes Trouble

BECOMING GAY EROTICA

ANGUS MACGREGOR

Sitting on this ridge top, I wonder why in the hell I ever agreed to come on this elk hunt. I don't really even like hunting. I used to, but not so much anymore. I mean, I love the camaraderie, and being outside in Oregon, and the beer. I love the beer the most. The whiskey is pretty great as well. I love the way the mist and clouds hug the mountains of the coast range like an old lady wearing a fur. The carpet of endless green, an ocean of Douglas fir that slides down the hills and tucks in and around rock outcroppings and pulls up its skirts for the rivers to splash through. The smell of wood smoke and the crisp autumn air that is just waiting to turn blue and bathe the mountains in frigid winter. But something is up with this hunting trip. It has been strange since the minute we got on the road. What am I saying? It's been weird for months.

Now that I am paying attention, and if I am honest, it's been going on since Emma and I met back in college. I dreaded the whole – "meet the parents" thing. I'm a real outgoing guy, not shy in the least. I don't have any confidence issues either. I mean, I'm lucky enough to have good looks and the kind of personality that most people seem comfortable with. But it's different meeting the parents. There's a whole other level of scrutiny and judgment that be part of that.

But I should back up, because this story began months before that, shit, it was years. I was the baby of my family, Chad Alonzo Martinez. A big brown-eyed, black haired, tanned little ball of energy. I had a brother that was ten years older than me. I adored him, but he and I had zero in common and hardly spent any time together at all. I was barely in grade school when he was graduating from high school. I did get to spend about a year in his bedroom before he moved out. See, I had a sister too, and she and I had shared a bedroom for quite a while, but as she got older, she was done with having a younger brother in the middle of her business. Jack said he didn't mind, which looking back, I find hard to believe. He was practically a grown man and I was just this cute little boy. But back then, I went to bed so early, he was rarely in the room with me. He came to bed way after me and I was always up and out of the room before he starts stirring since he didn't have a first period class.

There were a few nights I woke up in the middle of the night to look over and see him stroking his cock fast and furious. I knew better than to interrupt something so obviously private. But I would lay still and watch in fascination as his hand moved silently up and down his huge penis. His eyes would close and he would fondle his balls, belly, and nipples as he jacked. A few times, I even saw him seemingly slide a finger up his ass, which was both mystifying and utterly shocking at the same time. In the end, he would raise his furry ass off the mattress and send a fat rope of semen blasting up on his hairy chest and belly. He would usually grab some scandalously grimy cum rag from underneath the bed and wipe off his chest and then turn over and begin to snore. I had no idea what the whole thing meant, but it was fascinating nonetheless. A few years later, I followed in his footsteps and began rubbing one off every night before sleeping, secretly thinking my older brother for the lesson he didn't even know he was providing.

There were a few conversations that also contributed to my sexual education. Jack tended to take really long showers, probably because he was masturbating the whole time in there as well. Very often, I would be brushing my teeth or taking a little boy dump when he would open up the curtain and step out of the shower in all his muscled, hairy glory. Most often, his penis would be still erect and I would watch astonished as it bobbed and bounced on top of impossibly huge testicles. Several times he caught me watching and made a point to walk over and rub my face in his crotch, playfully, but all the same, shocking for a little kid. Sometimes he would reach down and grab my penis or nuts and give them a playful squeeze and say, something ridiculous.

"Damn, little bro, your dick is almost as big as mine. You are gonna be hung like a horse by the time you are in high school."

If you enjoyed this sample then look for **Here Comes Trouble**.

Also by this Author:

From the Author

Check my blog for Updates and interesting info.

Author Blog - angus-macgregor.awesomeauthors.org

If you enjoyed any of my books then please share the love and click like on my books in Amazon.

If you write me a review and send me an email I will send you a free book, or many.
(Just know that these emails are filtered by my publisher.)

Good news is always welcome.

One Last Thing, For Kindle Readers...

When you turn the page, Kindle will give you the opportunity to rate this book and share your thoughts on Facebook and Twitter. If you enjoyed my writings, would you please take a few seconds to let your friends know about it? Because... when they enjoy they will be grateful to you and so will I.

Thank You!

Angus MacGregor
angus_macgregor@awesomeauthors.org

About the Author

Angus MacGregor resides with his family in Oregon and Hawaii. Along with his passion for writing, Angus enjoys growing orchids, snorkeling and hiking.

Angus has worked as a school teacher, a financial analyst, and a small business developer. He currently works as a writer and supports firefighting efforts by working on wildfires in the US during the summer months. In addition to his adult erotica books, Angus has recently completed his first book of mainstream fiction.

"I love seeing what the Universe has in store for me as I create this reality. I love my life and the blessings of all the people and gifts that surround me. I wish peace and blessings to all my readers."